Portrait of a Sunset

JESSICA SCOTT ROMANO

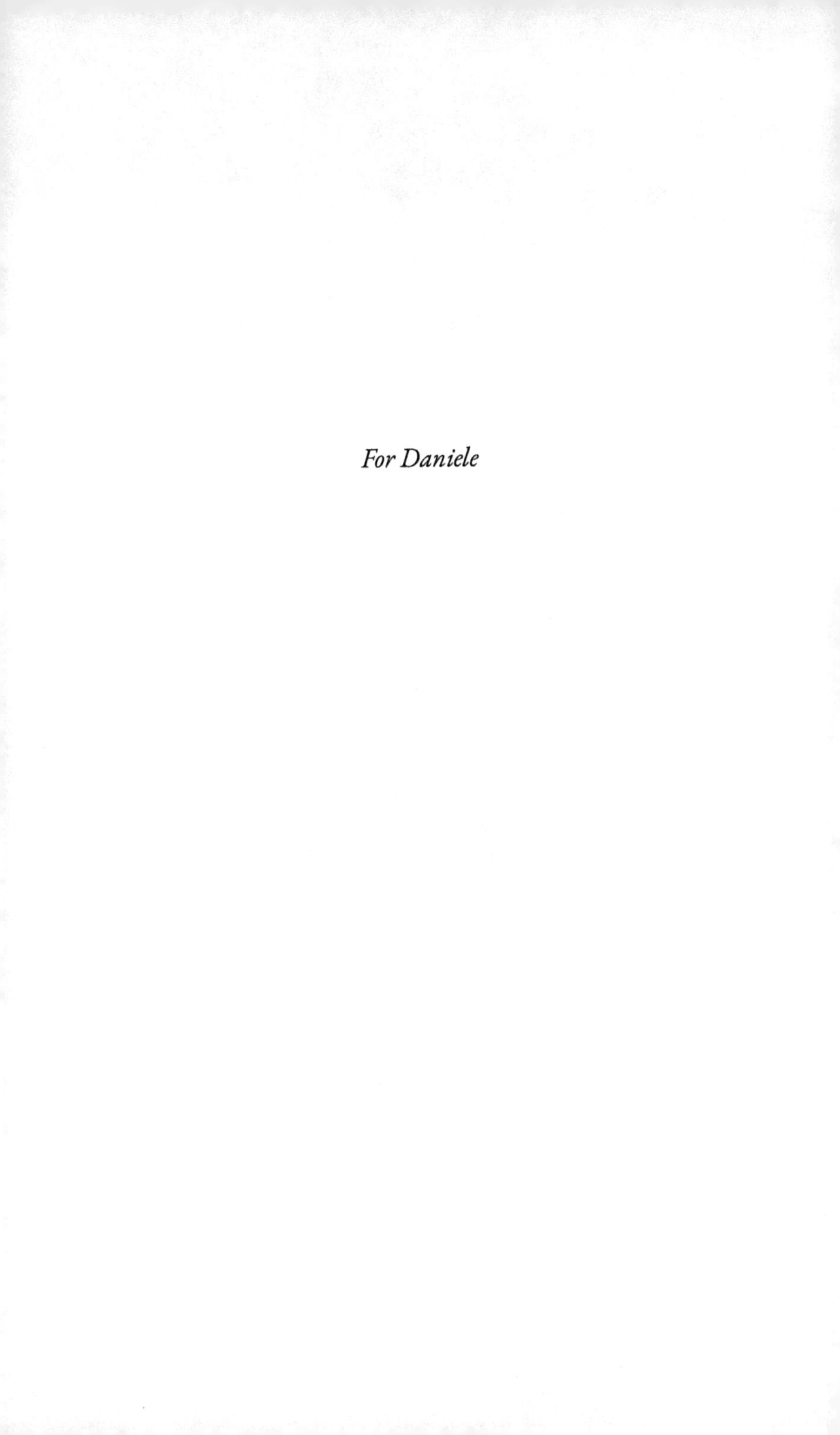

For Daniele

When I met Casey Linderman, I was a shell of the person I used to be—or worse: a shell of the person that I thought I should have been. A disastrous summer had ripped me out of my comfortably mediocre life as an artist in training and had thrust me into a world where I no longer belonged, a world in which I was completely, utterly, terrifyingly alone.

The worst part was, I was beginning to like it that way.

That was why, when I took a seat next to Casey in the first of many, many hospital-mandated group therapy sessions in the basement of the local YMCA, I didn't say a word. To my satisfaction, he didn't say one either.

I studied my worn-out tennis shoes as the other group members trickled into the oddly bright, strangely sanitary-smelling room. With weary eyes, I traced my dusty, fraying shoelaces as they looped around each other and formed a haphazard, off-white bow before coming to rest atop the graying canvas of the once-white sneaker.

Interesting.

I shifted to a less-slouchy position in my cold metal chair and checked my watch.

Five to seven. Therapy would be starting any minute. My stomach bubbled with nerves as I closed my eyes, trying to figure out how a girl like me had ended up in a place like that.

I took a deep breath and let it out. I could hear muttering around me as other people filled in the remaining empty seats. I tuned them out as I continued to try to calm down.

Just breathe, Clara, I told myself, *you can do this.*

I took another breath, focusing on the glow of the fluorescent lights coming through my heavy eyelids. I hadn't slept for three days. Subsequently, I began to drift off, my head drooping down onto my chest.

That's when the waves began to wash over me, softly at first, but steadily growing in power and succession until all at once they were crashing into me, stealing my breath as I fought the urge to scream. I could just see the sun, that false idol of hope and happiness, impossibly bright as it stared down at me dispassionately and I sank deeper and deeper into the depths of the darkening water.

I awoke with a jerk, stomping my foot and startling Casey, but no one else.

"Sorry," I muttered, wiping my eyes. I shouldn't have been surprised to find them wet with the beginnings of what was sure to have been a veritable torrent of tears, as per usual.

Casey grunted wordlessly in reply.

I decided to study his shoes for a while. Being a person who carefully avoided eye contact on most occasions, I learned a lot about people from their shoes. Take nurses, for example. On average, nurses wear sensible but stylish tennis shoes that give them the mobility to get where they are needed fast, but also afford them the opportunity to express their own individuality in terms of color and style. The nurses that work in pediatrics and love babies and puppies and all other cute, precious things usually wear pink-accented shoes, as well as their hearts on their sleeves. The serious, no-nonsense nurses in the Intensive Care Unit wear black tennis shoes to show that, whatever they're doing, they give it their all, and there will be no fooling around. Priests also wear black sneakers to display their commitment to their vows of poverty and modesty, and perhaps as a reference to the darker side of humanity that even a man of God must possess. Funeral directors wear shiny, impersonal, black loafers to signify that they do not want to share in your pain or be given any information about your plight because they have already heard it all before.

By that point in my life, I was an expert at shoe psychology. I could learn everything I needed to know about a person before I ever looked up at their face. Just by glancing at their footwear, I could tell who they were and where they were going—and how that would affect me.

Casey's shoes, though, were a complete enigma. They were huge, muddy, black, combat-style boots with thick soles and a good arch—great for walking and motorcycling and other general bad-assery. However, looped tight around one of the flat, black shoelaces on his boat-sized right boot was a single plastic purple flower on a string that looked as if it had come off a little girl's hair barrette.

Interesting.

"Welcome, everyone," called a gratingly cheerful voice from the front of the room. Reluctantly, I put my shoe-study on hold and looked up to see the grief counselor enter the room, closing the door behind him as he trapped us all in that brightly lit, white-walled lobby of hell.

He looked just as I thought he would: annoying.

Everything about him screamed "LOVE ME!"; from his green and black checkered sweater vest and matching chartreuse bowtie to his lime-colored dress shirt and fabulous, neon-green converse sneakers. His brown hair was parted on the left with a severe crease, and flecks of grey were just beginning to crop up around his temples, where I half-expected to see the remnants of some white clown make-up. He practically danced over to sit across from me in the circle of chairs, and picked up a clipboard from the floor under his seat, crossing his legs daintily.

"I'm so glad that you're all here," he said, nearly bursting the faux buttons on his sweater vest in his enthusiasm. "Welcome to the first official meeting of the Siblings of Homicide Victims Therapy Group!"

I winced. Not only had the ridiculously-perky therapist just reminded me of all that I had lost, but he had said those words so flippantly, so carelessly, as if they were just words and meant nothing.

But of course they didn't, really. Not to him, anyway.

Casey shifted uncomfortably in the chair to my left and I knew that I wasn't the only one who had been stung.

"Well, as you know," the counselor continued, "I am Doctor Jay Hartman, but you can just call me Doctor Jay. Let's go around the room and introduce ourselves, what do you say?"

No one said anything.

I took a look around the room at the twelve other zombie-like figures and was mildly surprised to find that I was not the only one with dark circles under my red, watery eyes, and I was not the only one who thought that "Dr. Jay" was turning out to be a colossal douche.

"Who wants to go first?" the "doctor" asked, beaming expectantly at each of us in turn. One by one, the group members' weary, bloodshot eyes dropped to the floor, hiding their pale, haggard faces from the counselor's view.

"Aww, a little shy, are we?" Jay asked, a subtle note of impatience coloring his effeminate voice. When no one replied, he continued, "Okay then, how about this: you all break into groups of two—"

My stomach sank. I hated groups of any size.

"—and interview each other? No topic is off limits. Remember, we're here to share our feelings!"

I felt like I might vomit. I barely acknowledged my feelings myself; I sure as hell wasn't ready to share them with anyone else. I closed my eyes again and took a deep breath. Like clockwork, the waves began to ebb and flow anew, and I wrenched my eyes back open.

"Do you want to be my partner?" I asked Casey's shoes, my voice rough as my panic slowly subsided.

He grunted again.

Not sure if that grunt meant yes or no, I glanced up and finally got my first real look at the man-mountain that was Casey Linderman. His broad, muscular shoulders were slumped in his blue flannel shirt, a posture that should have made him seem less like a giant, but somehow made him look even more gargantuan, making me wonder how the spindly metal chair beneath him could possibly be supporting his weight.

He had to have been at least six foot five, standing, and easily weighed 300 pounds or more, every pound of which appeared to be solid muscle. He looked too big to be allowed, as if he were some sort of mythical giant that, for whatever reason, had condescended to take a break from his normal routine of skull-crushing and monster-stomping to climb down his beanstalk and fraternize with us mere, grief-stricken mortals here on Earth.

I realized that my mouth was hanging open as I gazed up at his dark-complected face. His black, shaggy hair and five o'clock shadow made him seem all the more dangerous, but neither of those things could compare to his eyes. His fierce, haunted, blazing brown eyes glared down at me, as if they were trying to bore into my brain, as if he were challenging me to comment on his size like I am sure so many others had before.

I politely declined that challenge.

"I...I'm Clara Halpert," I stuttered, looking back down at my own weathered shoes.

"Casey Linderman," he rumbled in reply. His voice was so deep that I could feel my chair vibrate beneath me when he spoke.

"Come on, guys!" Jay cawed over the muted din, "You have to

talk! Why else would you be here? Now turn your chairs to face each other and let's get started!"

Suppressing a heavy sigh, I stood up and turned my chair to face Casey, who did the same.

"Um...I don't know what to say," I admitted quietly, my face flushing as I looked down at my hands. Eye contact had been difficult for me all of my life, but never more so than after the events of that summer.

"Me neither," Casey replied, clearing his throat uncomfortably.

After a brief inner-struggle with shyness, I looked up to meet his eyes again and was surprised to see that the giant looked just as nervous as I felt.

Interesting.

"Well, I guess I could ask you how old you are," I muttered, trying to sound off-handed.

"Twenty-three," he said shortly, "You?"

"Twenty. Do you go to school?"

"Not anymore. You?"

"Not really," I replied vaguely.

My palms were beginning to sweat. Already we were getting too close to the heart of the issue.

"Do you have a job?" I asked, my voice much too loud.

It was his turn to get uncomfortable. For some reason I couldn't discern, he began to fidget with the cuffs of his sleeves. "Um...not really, anymore."

I nodded, ignoring the fact that his answer was just as vague as the one I had given.

"Okay, guys," Jay said, barely having to raise his voice to be louder than the group, "now that you're all warmed up, I want you to tell your partner what brings you here to this group meeting tonight. I know it's hard, but the first step to overcoming your grief is to share it with someone else."

I glared at him.

Why was it that the most logical, poignant thing he'd said all night was exactly the thing that I least wanted to hear?

Casey cleared his throat again, and the people around us quietly began to share their deeply repressed pain with their partners. I looked up at Casey, panicking. The room began to spin as I was overcome with nausea.

"Do...you wanna go first?" Casey asked, looking a bit alarmed by my trembling and sweating as I hurtled toward a full-blown anxiety attack.

I shook my head. "I think I—"

"Hey, guys!" Jay crowed right in my ear. Casey and I both jumped. "I don't hear any sharing yet!"

"We're getting to it," Casey said, a bit brusquely.

"Well, how about you go first, little lady?" Jay suggested, picking up a strand of my long, curly hair and tossing it playfully back over my shoulder.

I couldn't look at him. I couldn't speak. My throat was tight and my stomach was squirming as if I'd just eaten a bucket full of worms. The room was spinning and I couldn't stop it. I couldn't talk about this, not yet. Not here. Not with Jay's strangely moist breath in my face.

"Go on," said Jay's muffled voice in my ear, "look your partner in the eye and tell him what you're feeling inside."

After trying and failing to catch my breath, I did as that douchebag counselor instructed. I stared right up into Casey's wide, fearful eyes and said, "I feel like I'm gonna be sick."

With that, I slumped over and vomited spectacularly, setting Dr. Jay's lovely lime-green sneakers adrift in a sea of sick.

"Oh! My! *GOD!!*" he shrieked, in the voice of an eight-year-old girl.

He finally leapt out of the way, but I could not stop painting the floor with what little I had eaten over the past twenty-four hours—and then some. My face grew hot and sweaty as I retched, my hair swinging dangerously close to the fountain of vomit.

Then, suddenly, I felt a rush of cool air as someone swept my long, loose curls out of the danger zone and gathered them up, holding them together at the nape of my neck as they rested their other hand on the small of my back. No one had touched me so tenderly in months, and no stranger had ever been that thoughtful toward me.

The surprise I felt must have overridden my brain's panicked instructions to my heaving stomach for, after what had felt like ten minutes, I was finally able to stop puking and come up for air. Too exhausted to feel embarrassed, I wiped my stinging lips on my jacket sleeve and sat up to face the rest of the group.

I had expected to see thirteen pairs of wide eyes staring at me in disgust, but instead saw only a haphazard half circle of empty chairs. I wiped my streaming eyes and turned, with some trepidation, to see who, if anyone, was still holding my hair.

It was Casey.

Giant, awkward, scary Casey was holding my hair and not looking disgusted at all. If I had been capable of feeling love at that moment, I would surely have fallen in love with him on the spot.

"Thanks," I said thickly, pulling a ponytail holder from my skinny wrist and gingerly taking my hair back from him.

He shrugged.

"Where did everyone else go?" I asked, forgetting to stare at his feet instead of his face.

"Dr. Jay ran out as soon as your puke hit his shoes," Casey said in a baritone monotone, "and everyone else took that to mean that Group was over."

I nodded, resting my aching forehead on my hand as I tried not to look at the mess I had made on the white linoleum floor. Then a thought swam into my foggy brain, and I turned back to Casey.

"Why didn't you leave, too?" I asked, suspicious.

He shrugged again, still fighting to pull the cuffs of his stubborn sleeves down over his own wrists. "I didn't have anywhere else to be just then."

Chapter Two

THAT NIGHT, I went home to my empty apartment, as usual.

Once inside, I felt my way over to the couch without turning on the lights. Wrapped in that all-too-familiar blanket of darkness, I kicked off my shoes and stretched out across the battered old cushions. My eyes ached with tiredness and my throat still stung from the vomit, so I lay back against the armrest and closed my eyes. I cashed in what few chips I had left and took a gamble on the man upstairs, praying that, for one night out of the eighty-seven and a half I had spent since Charlotte's death, I could sleep in peace without having to relive that horrible day over and over again.

God must have been feeling generous, because the last thing I saw before I gave in to the sandman was not the murky water washing over me, or my sister's lifeless eyes or her murderer's arrogant, taunting grin.

It was, oddly enough, the face of Casey Linderman.

Chapter Three

I AWOKE over sixteen hours later to the bright afternoon sun beating down on my face as it poured through the window and into my tiny living room. Groggily, I sat up and yawned. Normally, after a sleep coma like that one, I would awaken feeling even more exhausted than I had before, but that day was different. I didn't know why, but something had changed. Maybe it was the sunshine, or the sleep, or the fact that I'd finally achieved my dream of a dreamless night, but whatever it was, I actually felt like a human being for once, instead of a lifeless zombie.

Full of some vague purpose that I couldn't quite define, I stumbled down the shag-carpeted hall and into my closet-sized bathroom. Once my immediate needs were met, I stepped in front of the sink to wash my hands. As the cold water flowed into the even colder ceramic basin, I thought that, since I was already at the sink, I might as well brush my teeth—something I had recently been neglecting. There was no real reason to have fresh breath when the only people you ever spoke to were ghosts.

After giving my miraculously still-reasonably-pearly whites a thorough cleansing, I figured, since I was already in the bathroom,

I might as well take a shower too. Lord knows I didn't have anything better to do.

I undressed and stepped into the shower stall—I had deliberately rented an apartment without a bathtub—and closed the Plexiglas door behind me. Tentatively, I grasped the hot water faucet. I shivered a bit as the frigid apartment air clawed at my naked skin.

"Just turn on the water, Clara," I told myself, my voice rough from disuse. My hand trembled, so I gripped the tap tighter, clenching my teeth. I was sick of having the same argument with myself every time I had to use water. The bigger the faucet, the harder the struggle. But the water wasn't my enemy. The water hadn't killed my sister; she had been dead long before she had reached the bottom of that cold, heartless lake.

Tears sprang to my eyes and I realized that, as usual, it wasn't going to happen. I had lost. The shower had defeated me, and I was just going to go and cry myself into a stupor. Again.

I turned to open the shower door, my bare chest heaving with stupid, hiccupping sobs that sickened me. I glanced back at the showerhead, but it was no use. Already, visions of my sister's pale, swollen face were creeping up behind my eyes and I knew that I was in for yet another wasted day.

Depressed beyond recuperation, I stepped in front of the mirror above the sink and forced myself to take a look at what I had become. At one time, I had been proud of my long, chestnut-brown hair, but my once loose, lustrous curls had lost all of their shape, all of their shine. My eyes, my beautiful jade-green eyes, had faded to grey and had sunk into deep depressions in my skull, amidst painfully dark, purple shadows. My cheekbones stood out so far that I looked like a skeleton. My lips were cracked from dehydration and lip-biting, and my nose was dry and flaky from near-constant, crying-induced nose-blowing.

Who was that in the mirror? That girl wasn't me! At that moment I hated that grey-eyed stranger almost as much as I hated my sister's killer.

Suddenly filled with a rage I had never known before, I reached forward and grabbed the mirror by its frame and ripped it from the wall. Growling like a wild animal, I raised it above my head and turned to the shower—that damn, impenetrable shower—and I gathered my strength. Then, with a primal roar, I threw the mirror, sending it flying at the shower stall like a projectile missile. With sick satisfaction, I watched the looking glass shatter as it collided with the shower door, which exploded spectacularly, sending shards of splintered, tempered glass flying at me like a million tiny diamond bullets.

Miraculously, I was unhurt, but that only enraged me further.

I looked wildly around the room, searching for something else to break, to maim, to destroy. I wanted something, some unlucky inanimate object, to know what it was like to be so broken that there was no chance that it could ever be restored to what it had once been. Breathing heavily, I picked up the metal toilet paper rack (the only other thing in the room that wasn't bolted to the floor), and threw that at the shower stall too.

It bounced off the metal frame, doing no further damage.

The shower was mocking me.

Frustrated to the point of insanity, I screamed at the top of my lungs and I balled up my fist. Then, without as much as a millisecond of forethought, I punched the solid brick wall over the sink with all of my strength, shattering the bones in my right hand, but nothing else.

Instantly the rage left me and I collapsed onto the glass-ridden floor, clutching my broken hand, too shocked to scream or cry or even to regret my actions. As I began to lose consciousness, I remember thinking only one thing:

The shower had won again.

Chapter Four

A WEEK LATER, I was back at Group with a nifty neon-orange cast—a color the surgeon had said would "cheer me up" after my encounter with the nasty "burglar" that had attacked me in my bathroom. I took a seat by the door and examined the rows of plaster on my cast, feeling ashamed that I hadn't even had the guts to own up to what I had done to myself. In my defense, though, I had enough problems already. I didn't need to do a stint in a mental institution as well.

Or did I?

I was just beginning to realize the implications of my self-destructive behavior when someone plopped down onto the chair on my right.

I glanced over to see a very haggard-looking Casey look over at my cast.

"You okay?" he grunted, not meeting my eyes.

For a moment I was at a loss for words.

Was I okay? I had expected him to say something like "What happened?" or "How did you get the cast?" or, better yet, say nothing at all and pretend not to notice it. But what he had asked was different somehow, more personal.

"Yeah," I sighed.

His dark eyes darted to my face and I knew he didn't believe me. I also knew, however, that he was keeping just as many secrets as I was.

Just then, Dr. Jay entered the room, minus his previous enthusiasm. He threw me a sneer as he took a seat as far away from me as possible and said simply, "Just get into pairs again, everyone."

As people began to pair up and separate, he added, "And if someone needs to vomit, please do so in the restroom. My shoes still smell like stomach acid."

I frowned. I had not been aware that stomach acid had a distinctive smell. Nevertheless, I hung my head with what I hoped was an appropriate amount of shame and mumbled to Casey, "You wanna be partners again?"

"Will I need a poncho?"

I almost snapped my neck looking up at him, not sure I had heard him correctly.

"Did you just make a joke?" I asked, incredulous.

He shuffled his gigantic feet sheepishly as his dark face reddened. I felt an unfamiliar fluttering in my stomach, and I hoped that I wasn't about to throw up again.

"Maybe," he replied cryptically.

"Okay, same drill as last time," Jay called from across the room in a weary voice, "talk about what brings you here to Group. Really open up and share your feelings and blah, blah, blah."

Several people in the room gasped at his insensitivity, so he hastily added, "I'm kidding, of course! Trying to lighten the mood! Go ahead and talk amongst yourselves!"

Apparently I had broken Dr. Jay's spirit. All of his vim and vigor had disappeared, as had his fabulous wardrobe. Instead of a bright green sweater vest and painfully-bright sneakers, he was wearing a dull, brown knit sweater and drab, mocha-colored chinos with matching dress shoes.

Geez, you'd think he'd never been puked on before.

Casey cleared his throat awkwardly, and I rubbed my sweaty palm on my jeans as we both realized that it was time to get down to business.

"I'll go first this time," Casey said. I was sure he could see the beads of sour panic-sweat already forming on my burning forehead.

"Okay," I said, taking a deep breath, "what brings you to Group today?"

"My motorcycle," he said, giving me a strange look. It took me a moment to realize that there was only one word to describe that look.

Mischievous.

"Your motorcycle?" I asked, the corners of my mouth twitching as they fought off some strange force that was attempting to pull them upward.

"Yep," he nodded, casually crossing his arms over his chest. "I got on my motorcycle, started the engine, and it brought me here, of all places."

"It didn't know how to get to the mall?" I asked dryly, nearly losing my battle with the invisible strings pulling at the corners of my chapped lips.

He shrugged, the corners of his thin lips twitching as well. "I guess not."

"Well, since you're already here, I guess you might as well stay." I shrugged back.

"Yeah, I guess it's not the worst place to be...until someone pukes on your fruity green Converse."

I lost it. For the first time in months, laughter came spilling out of me even faster and more intensely than the vomit had. It started out quiet, but then it grew louder and louder until I was laughing so hard that my eyes were streaming and my ribs were aching.

"*HEY!*" Jay shouted, not daring to come within ten feet of the splash zone as he wagged a skinny finger at us, "This is a support group, not a comedy club, young lady! If you can't get it together, you can leave!"

Still giggling, I tried to put on a serious face as I muttered, "I'm sorry. Sorry, everyone."

Jay nodded huffily and went over to talk to another group, occasionally throwing dirty looks at me over his shoulder.

I turned back to Casey as my giggles finally subsided.

"Sorry about that," I breathed, rubbing my sore stomach, "I'm pretty sure I'm going crazy."

"You're not going crazy," Casey assured me. There was still a ghost of a grin on his face that told me that I wasn't the only one who was amused. "I'm pretty sure you're driving *him* crazy though."

I followed his nod to Jay, who was still snarling as he scribbled something on his yellow memo pad.

"That didn't take long," I said under my breath, utilizing my nearly atrophied facial muscles to smile at Casey.

"You two are supposed to be talking about your lost loved ones," hissed a voice from my left, startling me. It was a gaunt, grey-looking woman in her late sixties, who had paired up with the forty-something blonde next to us. Habitually, I looked down at her shoes, which were smart, simple black pumps, which told me that she was serious. I looked back up to see that her brows were knitted in disapproval as she continued, "Please respect the group. Believe it or not, some of us are actually here to heal."

That time, the shame with which I hung my head was genuine.

I had forgotten why I was there. I was there to talk about Charlotte, not to socialize, no matter how much better the latter made me feel.

"Okay," said Casey, sounding solemn, "let's get to it."

I glanced at him, a bit fearfully, as my stomach tightened.

"I am here..." He paused, and I suddenly realized that I was almost as afraid of listening to the dark secrets of his soul as I was of having to share mine. "I am here because...my little brother... was trampled to death by..." He took a deep breath, then exhaled as he finished with, "a herd of rabid unicorns."

I covered my mouth as I snorted. I could feel Jay's eyes on me as I struggled to compose myself. I fought to contain my silent giggles as Casey threw me a wink.

"That... must have been terrible," I wheezed, unable to stop a few giggles from leaking out.

"Oh, it was," he said with faux solemnity, "Little Sally never saw it coming."

"Your brother's name was Sally?" I asked, feigning surprise.

Casey grinned outright, his thin lips curving up into a smile that brought back my stomach flutters times ten.

"Well, yes," he replied, seeing the flaw in his story. "He was named after my great-great-grandfather, Sally Monica Maureen Joseph Linderman."

I burst with laughter again as Jay bellowed, *"REALLY?!?"*

"You're trying to get me in trouble!" I hissed at Casey, who had the audacity to give me another roughish wink as he leaned back and grinned in triumph.

Shortly after that, Jay decided to change tactics and read us a horribly morose poem about a boy whose twin sister had died at the hands of a serial rapist. After forty-something lines of see-through metaphors and shoddy slant rhymes, the boy ended up killing himself and whatever was left of my buzz.

The group dispersed with a flurry of jacket-donning and tear-wiping, and I was glad to get out into the crisp October air, even if I wasn't so glad to wave goodbye to Casey as I started down the sidewalk toward home.

Since Charlotte's passing, I had taken quite a liking to long walks. Unlike most people, who spent their walks pensively evaluating their lives and their past decisions and indecisions, though, I normally spent mine thinking about nothing but the hard concrete beneath my feet and the fierce wind chapping my face.

As I walked home that night, however, I broke my own rule of non-reflection to think back on my laughs with Casey. As the sharp nails of the cold wind scratched at my face and froze me to my very bones, I wondered if he was any warmer on his motorcycle.

Chapter Five

THE NEXT MORNING, I awoke with another new sensation in my stomach: hunger.

Perplexed by my sudden ravenousness, I shambled into my surprisingly well-lit kitchen as if I had never been in it before. I noticed the cabinets (whitewashed but faded), the countertop (beige and dusty), and a sink full of dishes I barely recalled using. Considering the fact that I had not eaten much more than a slice of bread or a few saltine crackers here and there during the previous few weeks, it was a wonder that I hadn't forgotten where I kept the real food.

Greedy for sustenance, I threw open one of the cabinet doors and rustled through my non-perishables until I found it—the Holy Grail of canned pastas: a family-sized can of Chef Boyardee Ravioli.

I was practically salivating as I rifled through the haphazardly arranged contents of my drawers to find the can opener. Hurriedly, I slapped the device onto the metal lip of the can and turned the knob on the side. As the silver lid pried itself away from the sides of the container, the aroma of the juicy marinara sauce inside nearly put me over the edge. It took all of my self-control to stop myself from eating the meat-filled pasta straight from the can. Beginning to drool, I dumped the ravioli into a dusty saucepan that had been sitting on my counter for a month and put it on the stove to cook.

I watched the floating pillows of pasta as a greedy wolf would watch its prey, waiting for just the right moment to pounce. Finally, after what felt like an eternity of slobber and stomach-grumbling, the sauce came to a boil.

I carelessly tossed a dishtowel onto the polished-oak table in the center of the kitchen and plopped the pan down onto it. The bottom had not even touched the cloth before I delved into the ravioli, using the large wooden stirring spoon to ram three piping-hot pockets of molten lava into my mouth.

I moaned in agony and banged the table with my cast as the scalding meat and cheese burned my lips and tongue, but I didn't dare spit it back out. The pasta tasted even better than it smelled, and I could no longer bear to miss out on something so wonderful, so delicious, so heavenly as that ravioli—Chef Boyardee's greatest creation.

To this day, I have never eaten another bite of food that has brought me even remotely close to the whole-body sensation that that old, likely out-of-date ravioli did. Although my body was thin and my stomach had shrunk, I ate the entire family-sized can. I even chased it with a heaping bowl of freezer-burned chocolate ice cream.

"Oh my God," I sighed as I lay on the couch a few minutes later, rubbing my distended stomach, "why did I ever stop doing that?"

Chapter Six

AFTER SIX DAYS of eating literally everything in my kitchen cabinets (including, I am ashamed to admit, a can of two-year old tuna fish) I returned to the group therapy session the following Monday in surprisingly high spirits. I had even attempted a rematch with my showerhead nemesis, and had (somewhat to my satisfaction) only spent an hour and a half crying afterwards. For the first time in a long time, I was full, I was clean, and I was ready to face whatever the day threw at me.

At least I was, until I found out what Dr. Jay had planned for us.

I took my usual seat next to the door, and I started to feel a bit paranoid when the other members of the group began to whisper amongst themselves and cast dark glances in my direction, obviously discussing what sort of shenanigans I would be getting into that day. I tried to ignore them and focus on quelling the ever-bubbling vat of anxiety that was my stomach as I waited for Casey to arrive.

As if on cue, Casey blew into the room like a silent storm and crashed down onto the chair next to me. My welcoming smile—

which, I confess, I had been practicing at home for days—fell as I felt waves of anger emanating from him like a tangible force field.

He looked awful.

I was not one to judge, but Casey looked even more haggard than I did, with his shaggy black hair in disarray and his five-o'clock shadow steadily growing into a ten-o'clock beard beneath his haunted, red-rimmed eyes. He slouched in his chair and held his left arm, the one closest to me, at an awkward, unnatural angle, as if he were trying to keep it from touching any other part of his body.

Interesting.

Every signal in my brain was shouting at me to just leave him alone, to look away at that moment before I got any more involved. I hadn't been interested in anyone else's problems since the "incident" at the lake, why should I start caring now? And why should I start with someone who was clearly as messed up—or possibly more so—than I was?

Nevertheless, curiosity got the better of me and I followed the sleeve of his long, brown, leather jacket from his broad shoulder to his thick wrist, where a thin trickle of blood was slowly sliding down onto his tightly-clenched fist.

"You're bleeding!" I gasped in a horrified whisper.

"Shut up!" he hissed back, so fiercely that he may as well have just slapped me in the face.

He glanced warily around at the other group members and used his clean hand to tug his sleeve down over his knuckles, and I fought an inner battle over whether or not to pursue the matter further.

I glanced over at him, my mouth open as if to speak, but his vicious glare killed the words before they could reach my lips.

I didn't know what he had done, but I was more than willing to bet that he had done it to himself. I looked dejectedly down at my own broken hand and wondered how I could have ever considered someone who was clearly as broken as I was to be an inspiration, inspiring me to eat tons of food and then to confront my showerhead enemy all because I had hoped to see him smile at me again. I had spent the past few days dwelling on the laughter he had shown me, but I had forgotten that I didn't actually *know* Casey; I didn't know anything about him at all.

What I did know, though, was that he had made me smile when I no longer thought that was possible, and that was good enough for me.

"I...if, if you hold it up above your heart," I said quietly, haltingly, "it should slow the bleeding."

Casey's stony façade softened a bit as he grunted and crossed his arm over his chest, as if he were scratching his right shoulder.

I felt a bit of a thrill as I realized that Casey thought my advice to be worthwhile, but that thrill immediately died when Dr. Jay entered the room and announced the day's agenda.

"Alright guys," he said, his previous peppy perkiness completely gone now, "today is the day that you share with the group how your sibling died. There will be tears and there will be anger and there will be pain, but the first step to acceptance is coming to terms with what happened. Who wants to go first?"

I bowed my head as my heart began to race. I could feel Jay's eyes on me as the room began to spin and the water began to seep into view behind my eyes. I couldn't do this. I wasn't ready!

I closed my eyes and took a deep a deep breath, trying to slow my rapidly increasing heartbeat. The only thing that I hated more than reliving my sister's death was the fact that I forced myself to do it so often. Now I would not only have to relive it again, but I'd have to do it in a room full of judgmental—or worse, pitying —faces.

Anxiety flooded my brain as I began to fidget with my clothes and bounce my knee up and down with nervous energy while a sixteen-year-old girl with dark hair across the circle started us off with the heart-wrenching tale of her brother, a third-grader at Most Blessed Sacrament elementary school, who was gunned down by a hostile gang member in an alleyway just for being in the wrong place at the wrong time. The sound of the girl's hollow, empty voice brought to mind my mother's numb eulogy at Charlotte's funeral, the voice of a woman who had lost everything, and had no hope of ever regaining it.

The room was running out of air as my chest compressed with the pressure of just living another day alone, not to mention sharing that sentiment with a group of total strangers. I began to beat my cast upon my bouncing knee in a desperate attempt to distract myself as the girl got to the point in the story in which she found her baby brother in the alley behind her house.

My heart pounded even faster as the water swam across my vision, taking me right back to that day at the lake. I could almost feel my lungs filling with the cold, murky water as I sat there in my chair, struggling to remember that it wasn't real, not anymore. I fought the urge to part my lips and gasp for air, shaking my knee faster and faster as the girl approached the lifeless body of her little brother in the alleyway and reached out with a shaky hand to turn him over, revealing his blank, bloody face.

Just then, Casey reached over and grabbed my shaking knee with his own bloody hand. I snapped out of my strange half-consciousness and looked over to see him as white as a ghost. I could feel a tremor in his large hand as he leaned in and whispered, "Let's get out of here."

His breath was hot in my ear and the depth of his voice gave me goose bumps, but it was the urgency in his voice and my own near-hysterical panic that caused me to nod hastily and let him take me by my good (albeit sweaty) hand and pull me to my feet.

The girl's voice faltered as we reached the door, but by then we were moving so fast that I didn't have time to feel guilty or rude. Hand in shaky hand, Casey and I raced through the hall and up the basement stairs, both trying to outrun the demons we wished we could have left behind us in that room.

Casey exhaled explosively as we burst out into the sharp, cold night air. I rubbed my stinging eyes and breathed deeply, trying to forget what I'd heard in that room and what I'd seen in my mind. I gasped for air as if I had truly been drowning, and I could hear Casey's own labored breathing a few steps behind me.

As my head cleared, leaving me with the familiar fatigue that always came after an intense anxiety attack, I glanced over at Casey, who was pacing back and forth, running his hand through his hair. I decided to give him a moment to collect himself, partially because that's what I would have wanted if it had been me, and partially because his agitation was really starting to scare me.

"GODDAMMIT!" he shouted suddenly, his voice echoing in the darkness of the YMCA parking lot.

I jumped and turned to see him clenching his left fist as blood streamed steadily down into a small red puddle on the sidewalk. My stomach squirmed at the sight of so much blood, but I pushed my selfish thoughts aside and rushed over to help him.

Timidly, I reached out for his hand. He tugged it out of my reach.

"Don't," he warned, his eyes wide and wild as he swayed unsteadily.

"I just want to look," I persisted. My voice was several octaves higher than usual, but my reassuring tone must have gotten across nevertheless, because he extended his thick arm out to me as he turned his head to look the other way.

I balanced the back of his forearm on my bulky cast and used my free, if somewhat clumsy, left hand to pull back his sleeve. I drew a sharp intake of breath through my teeth as I saw the long, dark, horizontal line of severed skin on his wrist, just below the heel of his hand.

"How bad is it?" Casey asked. I was alarmed to hear the tremble in his deep voice.

"Well, there's a lot of blood here," I admitted, giving myself time to make out how deep the gash really was.

Casey glanced over to look at his own cut and suddenly his

arm slipped out of my grip. His body jerked and his stomach heaved and he fell to his knees, vomiting violently onto the cold concrete sidewalk.

As I fell to my knees beside him, hurriedly digging in my jacket pockets for a clean tissue, I was aware of the odd irony of our newly-forming friendship. Apparently, we were unable to be stable people at the same time. However, the instability of one of us seemed to bring out the stability in the other.

Interesting.

I had never seen anyone vomit so much in my life. I had vomited pretty spectacularly myself on several occasions, especially lately, but Casey's body seemed to be attempting to rid itself of everything he had eaten in the past twelve years. Unable to do much but avert my eyes and try not to inhale the sickly-sour stench of stomach acid (Dr. Jay was right, it did have a distinctive smell), I rubbed Casey's back in a manner that I hoped came off as soothing and not creepy.

Finally, after several long, painful minutes, Casey took a ragged breath and sat down on the sidewalk, unable to move more than a few feet away from the contents of his stomach. His breathing was rough, and I handed him what I prayed was an unused Kleenex. He nodded in appreciation as he wiped the beads of sweat from his brow and dabbed at his wet lips.

I continued to rub his back, mostly because I didn't know what else to do for him. I hadn't comforted anyone else for months; I had forgotten what it was like to even have empathy for another living person until that moment. When it came to interacting with other people, I was out of practice, and I was hoping it didn't show.

"I can't..." Casey muttered moments later, not meeting my eyes, "I can't...look at blood." He glanced at me nervously, as if he were afraid that I would mock him for his weakness. "Ever since my little sister..." He looked away and gave a dry heave.

"Was trampled by unicorns?" I suggested, hoping my shy grin would inspire one in him.

He chuckled darkly and looked down at the flower on his boot. "Yeah."

I sat down next to him on the cold gray concrete and sighed as I said, "I know how you feel."

Casey finally looked at me. As his dark brown eyes searched my face for signs of the secret he knew I wasn't ready to share, I felt his sticky fingers fold around my hand.

"CLARA HALPERT!"

Casey and I both leapt to our feet as Dr. Jay shouted at us from inside the lobby of the YMCA. I knew that his once cheerful demeanor had been steadily morphing into a not-entirely-unreasonable disdain for me, but I had never imagined that he could look so angry. His round face was pink and puffy and his grey-checkered sweater vest was rumpled as he bore down on us, huffing and puffing like an angry bull.

I stood rooted to the spot, as if I had been petrified by Medusa. I half expected snakes to sprout from his neatly coiffed hair or smoke to spout from his rapidly reddening ears.

"Come here!" he shouted when he reached the glass doors.

"Run," Casey muttered under his breath, looking alarmed.

"What?" I asked, incredulous. Hadn't we already been caught? Where could we possibly go from there?

"Run!" he repeated, grabbing my hand again. Butterfly wings thudded weakly against my ribcage as he took off running, pulling me behind him.

I was too caught up in the moment to look back at Jay, but I could still hear him cursing like a sailor as he plodded along behind us, shouting something that sounded a lot like "I *will* help you, you ungrateful little pricks!" followed by the word "Shit!" as he ran through Casey's vomit, surely convinced that it was me who had ruined his shoes once again.

As suddenly as we had started, Casey and I stopped running

and I doubled over, gasping like a fish out of water as I clutched a stitch in my side. For a second, I was certain that I was dying from the sheer thrill of the moment, but then I realized that three months of moping and crying and lying on the couch had left me sorely out of shape.

"Get on," Casey ordered, throwing his leg over a large, shiny black motorcycle that had seemingly just appeared out of nowhere.

"What?" I repeated, this time with an agitation that had nothing to do with Dr. Jay bearing down on us like a freight train.

"Get on!" he shouted, looking at me as if I were an idiot. "What, have you never ridden a motorcycle before?"

I shook my head.

Half of my brain (the half that spoke in my mother's voice), was telling me to run back the opposite direction, that no good could come from hopping onto a motorcycle with a guy I barely knew.

The other half, however, was intrigued.

Casey looked conflicted as well. Then, with a heavy sigh, he said, "Okay, we don't have to if you don't want—"

"*I want!*" I squealed as Jay caught up to us, his flat grey converse sneakers slapping on the pavement like some kid's obnoxious swim fins. "Go go go!"

I scrambled onto the bike behind Casey and he started the engine.

"Hold onto me!" he shouted over the deafening roar and the rumble that shook every atom of my body. I did as he said and wrapped my arms around his torso, gripping my cast with my left hand over his stomach.

With that, Casey gave it some gas and the motorcycle lurched forward at breakneck speed, leaving both my stomach and my doubts behind us in the parking lot with Jay.

Chapter Seven

As we drove off into the night, I had no idea where we were going, but I was in no hurry to get there. Something about the rumbling of the bike beneath me and the cold wind blowing my hair made me feel more alive than I had ever felt. Every single molecule in my body was tingling and the butterflies in my stomach seemed to be having some sort of rave.

Being so close to Casey didn't hurt either.

Though the night air was frigid, Casey kept me warm. His leather jacket was unzipped, and through my thin jacket sleeves I could feel his tense, taut stomach as it moved slightly forward and backward as he took deep, slow breaths to calm his nerves. I had never been that close to another person, not even before Charlotte's death. It was as if the two of us had melded into one being as soon as my arms had encircled his waist, and it wasn't difficult to delude myself into thinking that he and I had a connection; maybe even a future.

As we sped past a row of parked cars, I rested my cheek on his back and closed my eyes. As I breathed in the smell of warm leather and exhaust fumes, I almost forgot, for a moment, to be afraid.

Chapter Eight

ABOUT FIFTEEN MINUTES after leaving our therapist screaming in the parking lot of the YMCA, I felt the motorcycle slow to a stop and my heart sank. The ride was over. We had escaped. Casey would tell me to catch the next bus and I'd go home to my dark, lonely, haunted apartment and try to forget that there was anything more to life than crying and reliving the past.

Casey shut off the engine and the silence of the city pressed against my ears like a woolen blanket. Reluctantly, I released my death-grip on Casey's waist and looked around.

We were in another, much smaller, parking lot in front of a dilapidated mechanic's garage. The windows of the small, square, squatty building had been broken in several places, as if someone had thrown rocks through them, and garbage littered the ground, blowing listlessly across the concrete in the slight breeze. As I watched, a few flecks of the dull grey siding paint chipped away from the wall, floating in the air for a moment before falling to the ground like dirty snow. A crooked sign emblazoned with equally crooked, hand-painted black letters hung above the large, rectangular steel door and declared that that seemingly abandoned piece of rubble had a name.

"Linderman's," I read out loud as Casey dismounted the ticking and clicking motorcycle. "This is yours?"

"It is now," he replied, wiping some road dirt from his brow and accidentally smearing his face with blood from his hand.

"Wow," I marveled. No matter how shabby that little shack was, Casey owned it. I had never owned any kind of property in my entire life, especially not something that had been inherited from an earlier generation.

Casey chuckled.

Startled, I turned to see him grinning down at me as if I were some sort of strange but endearing oddity that had just shown up on his doorstep, like a sad, one-eyed kitten he almost wanted to pet.

"What?" I demanded, feeling self-conscious.

He shrugged. "Nothing. I've just never seen anyone look at this place like that before."

"Like what?"

I knew how I'd been looking at it, but I was hoping that my thoughts were less transparent than I thought they were.

He shrugged again. "Like it was important, like it was something special. To everyone else, it's just a pile of crap. The city's thinking of condemning it."

"Oh no!" I exclaimed, too loudly. I blushed and added, more quietly, "You can't let them do that."

"I won't," he assured me, extending a clean hand to help me off the motorcycle. I took it and was a bit alarmed when my feet hit the ground and my legs began to rattle and vibrate beneath me. I feared for my balance, and I gripped Casey's big hand tighter. To my surprise, he laughed again.

"I forgot," he grinned as I scowled up at him indignantly, cursing the height difference that made me feel like a silly little child, "You've never been on a bike before."

"So?" I was really getting scared. My legs were so unsteady that I felt as if they were going to collapse beneath me, and my hypochondriacal brain interpreted this as a symptom of an oncoming medical disaster. But still, Casey laughed.

"*So*," he said, breaking my claw-like grip on his hand and putting his arm around my emaciated waist, "it takes a while to readjust to being on solid ground after you get off a bike, especially the first few times. Your body gets so used to the rumbling of the engine that your legs get confused when they get back on the ground."

I frowned doubtfully and he chuckled.

"You just have to walk it off, that's all," he said, his voice gentle. With that, he began to steer me toward the steel-plated garage door and I was powerless to resist. Step by shaky step, I walked with Casey to what very well could have been some sort of murder house for all I knew. He could have been leading me right up to the gates of Hell itself, but at least he wasn't sending me home. There was something about the ease of his embrace and his adorable smile, as lopsided as the sign above my head, that made me feel... something. I wasn't quite sure how to label this newfound emotion yet, but I was more than willing to do some more research on the subject.

I leaned into his torso, pinching a piece of his leather jacket between my sweaty fingers, and he escorted me through a smaller steel side door that I hadn't noticed before.

"Voila!" he said with a flourish as he flipped on a light switch, bathing the large, square room with a dim, flickering yellow light.

I had never been inside a mechanic's garage before, but it looked exactly as I had imagined it would. It seemed to be composed of floor-to-ceiling concrete, with shelves full of rusty gears and other metal doo-dads running along two of the four white-painted walls. The floor was covered in various piles of other mechanical-looking odds and ends, and in the center of it was a large, shiny metal car lift, embossed with the same name that hung on the sign outside.

"What do you think?" Casey asked, sounding a bit nervous as

he took off his jacket with some difficulty and hung it on a hook near the door. "I mean, it's not much, but—"

"It's awesome," I said, with about eighty percent honesty. "Do you know how to use all those tools?" I was a bit awestruck as I pointed to an enormous metal toolbox in the corner piled high with drills, screwdrivers and a bunch of other things I couldn't have identified if my life depended on it.

"Of course," he replied, a smidgeon of pride seeping into his voice as he steered me farther into the room, "No mechanic's son could go through life without learning the trade, whether he wants to or not. How do you think I keep my bike soooo..."

"*Soooo...* what?" I asked as he trailed off, his voice slurring. "Casey?"

"Nothing, I'm fine," he said, his loud voice booming in my ears and echoing off of the thick walls, "I just looked at the blood again, that's all. I'm—"

What he was, I will never know. I had just enough time to look up and into his chalk-white face before his big brown eyes rolled back in his head and he collapsed, losing consciousness as he fell on top of me, crushing me into the cold steel of the car lift.

"Casey!" I squeaked, my own voice surprisingly shrill, considering that he was crushing my windpipe. Five-foot-seven, 105-pound pseudo-skeletons are not built to support the dead weight of six-foot-six, three hundred-plus pound men—it's just physics! Thank God I'd eaten four microwave burritos for lunch every day that week, or I wouldn't have even lived to tell the tale.

"Casey, come on," I grunted. The greater part of his flannel-clad stomach was lying so heavily on my cast that I swore I could hear the plaster begin to splinter. "Oh, God," I muttered to myself, trying to squirm out from under him.

I had thought about dying a lot since the day I lost Charlotte, but none of the scenarios I had envisioned involved being crushed to death by a giant. In his defense, though, he was quite an adorable, sweet (but still adequately bad-ass) giant, so I had to admit that it would not have been the worst way to die.

Summoning my newfound, burrito-fueled strength, I put my miraculously-free left hand under Casey's right arm (which was, awkwardly enough, crushing my breasts up into my collarbone) and shoved the upper half of his body aside, freeing my chest and my broken hand. Panting with exertion from an act that an able-bodied person probably could have done without breaking a sweat, I glanced down to make sure that my cast was still intact. I cursed as I saw that there was a long, thin split running along the inside of my palm from my thumb to my wrist.

Trying not to think about how I would explain that to the ER doctor with the all-too-knowing eyes, I wriggled the rest of my body out from under Casey, who mumbled something unintelligible. As I rubbed the cast over my throbbing hand (as if that could somehow lessen the pain beneath it), Casey's mumblings got louder, but not much clearer.

"Rumsfeld," he said. (At least, that's what I heard anyway.)

"What?" I panted, baffled.

"Rosen."

"I don't understand," I said, getting a bit annoyed. First he had almost crushed me to death, and now he was speaking in tongues. "Casey, I don't—"

"ROSIE!" he bellowed suddenly, bolting into an upright position so fast that I screamed and slid backward across the floor in an instinctual effort to get away from him.

As I cowered against the almost comically large toolbox in the corner, Casey turned to me, his wild eyes blazing with an intensity that shook me to my very core. I had to cover my mouth with my hands so that I wouldn't scream again.

"Clara," he exhaled explosively, much like he had outside the YMCA. He sounded relieved to see that it was just me, but that scared me even more. What the hell kind of inner demons was he grappling with if he was relieved to see someone like me?

"Are...are you...alright?" I asked hesitantly, as he laid back down on the cold metal car lift, covering his eyes with his hand as his broad chest rose and fell in quick succession.

"Yeah," he grunted, his face waxy and his hair wild.

I was not convinced.

"I'll go get something to clean up all the bl—I mean, your arm," I said, getting up. My legs felt shaky again, but this time it had nothing to do with riding a motorcycle.

"There are some rags in the storage closet," he said without uncovering his eyes, "There's a sink in there too."

I nodded in spite of the fact that he wasn't looking at me, then I scurried toward one of three tall, rectangular metal doors along the back wall of the blocky room, making sure to give Casey a wide berth in case he felt the need to jump up and call out another woman's name again. As I turned the rusty round doorknob on the door labeled "STORAGE," I stepped into a small, dark washroom that looked a lot like the janitor's closet from my middle school. I could just make out the shapes of several broom or mop sticks and a few buckets, but it took me a few minutes of blind groping to find the small pile of rags in the back corner. Feeling a bit spooked, I grabbed four or five without really looking at them and wetted two in the bulky, stained industrial sink before practically running back out into the slightly-better-lit workroom of the garage.

"You find 'em?" Casey inquired groggily. He was still lying on the floor in the same position he had been in when I left. I stopped for a moment as I watched his thick chest rise and fall, more slowly now, and I was struck by the intense vulnerability of such a big, burly man. "Clara?" he prodded.

"What? Oh, yeah, I found them," I replied, snapping out of my inappropriately timed reflection on human nature. "Just keep your eyes closed," I instructed, kneeling down and taking his bloody left hand in mine.

"You got it, boss," he replied, sounding weary.

Very slowly, I peeled back the blood-caked sleeve of his red flannel shirt and exposed the skin from his hand to his inner elbow, revealing a dark, sticky mess. I looked away for a moment, fighting the urge to vomit as I inspected the round fluorescent lamps hanging from the ceiling.

"You okay?"

I looked back down to see Casey staring at me worriedly, though I couldn't tell whether he was more concerned for me or for himself.

"You're supposed to be keeping your eyes closed," I reminded him, trying to smile but failing. Smiles are difficult enough for a grief-stricken girl to manage on her own without throwing blood and gore into the mix.

"Sorry, boss," he said, trying to smile and succeeding. He closed his eyes, resting his free hand on his stomach.

Faced with no other option, I looked back at his wrist and thought through my plan of action out loud.

"I think I'll just wipe away the blood first..."

"Please don't tell me about it," Casey groaned, his deep, rumbling voice bordering on a whine.

"Oh yeah, sorry."

Without another word, I took one of the wet rags and gently cleared away the blood from around the razor-thin cut. I bit my lip as Casey inhaled sharply.

"Sorry," I repeated, miserable. I was not a nurse. I wasn't qualified for wound-cleaning of that caliber!

"Don't be sorry," he said, reaching up and awkwardly patting my shoulder with his free hand. (How he found my shoulder without opening his eyes, I don't know). "The whole thing's my fault anyway."

"What happened?" I asked quietly, sure that the question was too personal.

Casey took a long pause while I dabbed at the cut, which was still oozing crimson goo even though I had already wiped away two rags' worth of it from the rest of his arm.

"I found my baby sister's blanket today," he said finally. His voice was strange, as if there were something in his throat trying to block the words from escaping. I stopped trying to wrap his wrist in a rag-bandage to listen. Just like I had been at Group, I was almost afraid to hear his story. "It was in the storeroom with Dad's rags."

A horrible thought crossed my mind and I glanced down at the two rags I hadn't used. One was a rough, green, wool swatch and the other looked like a piece of an old grey t-shirt.

"She had been looking for it for months, but he'd cut it up, that bastard, and all but one square of it was covered in motor oil and grease."

I looked down at the rag I had tied around his wrist. Brown. Not a baby blanket.

"I was so pissed at him then, that he could do that to Rosie, the little girl who had loved him for six freaking years!"

I glanced at the first rag I had used, my heart pounding in my throat.

Grey t-shirt.

"I mean, God, she had carried it with her everywhere since she was old enough to walk! She used to sit on my lap and tell me stories about the little pink bunnies on it."

I looked at the last rag and felt my leaden stomach sink to my knees. It was purple and covered with blood...and little pink bunnies.

"Oh no," I whispered, pulling my hands up to my mouth again.

"I know," he continued, misinterpreting my statement, "What kind of monster would destroy a kid's blanket like that?"

"Me."

"What?"

"Open your eyes," I told him, as tears sprang to mine. What had I done? Why hadn't I looked at the rags?

I picked up the scrap of blanket by its corner and held it up for Casey, whose face changed from white to red so fast that I thought he might pass out again.

"I didn't look at it," I tried to explain, my voice small as he sat up and ripped the ruined rag from my hand and stared down at it, horrified, "I didn't know it was a blanket, I just—"

"You just destroyed the only thing I had left of my sister," he said, a current of barely controlled anger rippling beneath his voice.

I tried to grab for the blanket, but he snatched it away from me and held it to his chest.

"Maybe we can fix it," I suggested desperately, "I can wash it and—"

"No, you can't *wash it*, and you sure as hell can't *fix it*, Clara!" he said, mocking my now-squeaky voice, "It's ruined, just like every other goddamn thing I own!" He threw the blanket on the floor and got to his feet.

As I knelt on the floor, he stormed over to the toolbox and kicked it as hard as he could, sending tools and scraps of metal spilling out onto the floor with such a cacophony of clattering that I was certain a neighbor would be calling the cops.

"Casey, I'm so sorry!" I shouted, really crying now, not because I was afraid of him—though I was—but because I knew that losing the last tie to a loved one was like feeling them leave you all over again.

I reached out to him but he kicked a drill at me, narrowly missing my right ankle.

"I wish I'd never brought you here," he spat, giving me a bitter look of pure and utter hatred that nearly shattered my battered heart. "I should have known you wouldn't understand. I shouldn't have felt sorry for you. I should have just left you at the YMCA, panting like a fish out of water and shaking like a freakin' Chihuahua!"

My guilt turned to hurt and anger as he crossed the line.

"You're a jerk," I said quietly, my voice deadly calm despite the river of tears still flooding my face. "I may have my problems, but at least I don't try to hurt people who are only trying to help me."

Seething with anger, I kicked the drill back at Casey's stupid, flowery combat boots and ran out the door, slamming it behind me and wishing, like him, that he had never brought me to that garage.

Chapter Nine

SCREW CASEY, I thought angrily, storming across the empty parking lot. I didn't need his pity! I didn't need his emotional baggage! Who was *he* to mock *me*? At least *I* didn't pretend to be funny and nice when I was really just a drill-kicking, blanket-worshipping asshole!

The further I got from Linderman's garage, the angrier I got. My once-wet cheeks had long since dried as I embraced the raw, blistering flame of righteous anger burning in my belly. I hadn't felt angry in months. I hadn't felt much of anything but numb or sad since Charlotte was killed, but now I felt furious. I felt livid. I felt alive.

I also felt hungry.

I stopped stomping across pitch-black yards and shadowy side streets long enough to locate the nearest convenience store, whose enormous neon sign was flickering like a lighthouse beacon on a nearby corner. Then, without slowing down, I rerouted my tornado of anger in that direction.

I entered the small, too-bright Thornton's gas station and threaded my way through the stumpy sunglasses displays and magazine racks to make a beeline for the snack aisle. Greedily, I snatched up four foot-long Slim Jims before heading over to the fountain drink dispenser and filling up a forty-four ounce Styrofoam cup with cherry Slushee. My anger dissipated as I took a sip of that wondrous, semi-frozen concoction, and I had to stop myself from running as I hurried back through the maze of mostly useless items to the register to pay for my dinner.

"That all?" the hefty cashier asked, not looking up from his own feast of three greasy cheeseburgers, each dripping with cheddar and onions and surrounded on all sides by a fortress of soggy yellow fries.

"Yes," I said, hoping he wasn't going to touch my Slim Jims. He was just as greasy as his food, with a fat face full of zits and a prematurely balding head that glistened with sweat in the overhead light as he punched in the prices of my items on the register with his pudgy, slippery-looking fingers.

"$3.69," he said in a monotone, and I pulled my small, frayed, Hello Kitty wallet from my back pants pocket and extracted my last four one dollar bills.

"You can keep the change," I told him, trying not to touch his fingers as I handed over the money.

"Sweet," he replied, stabbing a button that sent the cash drawer shooting out of the register without ever taking his eyes off of his burgers. "Have a good night."

"You too," I replied, without much enthusiasm.

He hadn't touched my beef jerky, but I wiped it on my pant leg anyway as I headed back out into the night. I secured my Slushee to my chest with my right elbow as I opened the first of the Slim Jims with my teeth, spitting out the small piece of detached plastic onto the gas station's craggy macadam.

Nearly salivating now, I snapped into the Slim Jim and moaned in satisfaction as the spicy almost-meat danced over my cold, cherry-flavored tongue.

Distracted by the deliciousness of my snack, I almost stepped right into on-coming traffic. Luckily, a man in an SUV honked his horn at me and brought me back to my senses. I waved my Slim Jim in apology and found the sidewalk, on which I froze.

Where was I?

I looked around, clutching my snacks to my chest in panic. I had not been paying attention to where we were going when Casey and I had been on the motorcycle, and I didn't recognize anything in my current vicinity. Aside from the brightly lit Thornton's, there was nothing notable about my surroundings at all. There was a short, raggedy-looking fence that led to an alley behind the store, and there was a multitude of ominous-looking trees, all black and menacing in the shadows that were made even darker by the gas station's almost-eerie white and blue lights. The cracked sidewalk on which I stood lead off to the left somewhere, maybe down a side road, maybe to a slaughterhouse, I didn't know. Just as the situation was growing more and more terrifying in my overactive imagination, a cold breeze blew, cutting right through my too-thin jacket and slicing into the bones beneath it.

Not knowing what else to do, I stopped standing there looking around like a lost tourist and began to walk purposely in what I thought might have been an eastwardly direction.

My beef jerky lost its taste as I power-walked toward something, anything that looked familiar. I went down a shady street and passed house after dark, dilapidated house, stepping on glass after broken glass, and my panic surged as I realized that I was on the "bad side" of town, the side my father had always warned me never to set foot in, even in the daylight. My family was not rich, but we were well-off enough to make my parents believe that the low-income part of town was something that they should shun, not even looking at it through their car windows as they drove past. I had always just assumed that their timidity was due to some sort of perceived financial superiority. However, now that I was alone and exposed, out in the open air of what my dad would call "the projects," crushing beer bottles and lord knows what else beneath my sneakers while broken-down houses shifted and settled further sideways as far as they possibly could without completely falling down in the strange, tense silence of the late evening, I was beginning to think that maybe there was something to their reluctance after all.

I jumped as I heard what I thought was a footstep behind me, but when I looked back, I saw nothing.

I was an idiot. I had heard enough stories of rape and murder to know better than to venture into an area like that alone at night, but there I was, all by myself and completely lost. I had been too busy sniffing Casey's jacket and feeling his abs to notice where he was taking me, and now I was paying the price.

I sped up slightly, darting from streetlight to streetlight, as if the dim, buzzing yellow bulbs would burn the lurking boogeymen and rapists into dust.

Then I saw it. A park. An almost pleasant-looking, bench-pocked park full of halogen lights and a beautiful concrete fountain shaped like an angel.

Almost running now, I rushed across a small, spooky alleyway and onto the grassy field, certain that I heard footsteps behind me, but not looking back.

Panting, I reached the foot of the fountain and looked up at the twelve-foot tall, graffiti-covered angel. She held a Bible in one hand and what looked like a sword handle in the other, and her face was serene as she looked out over the park with her blank stone eyes. Though she was sporting a broken nose and a chipped wing, she was still a symbol of hope for me in the cold, dangerous darkness. I wasn't overly religious myself, but how could an angel not be a good omen?

Looking back now, I have no idea why I thought I would be safe in an empty park at ten o'clock at night, or why I hadn't just stayed at Thornton's and asked for directions, or maybe even swallowed my pride and walked back to Casey's to ask him for a ride home. At that moment, though, I felt almost peaceful as I took a seat on a rusty, vandalized bench close enough to see the water in the base of the fountain, but not close enough to touch it.

Sipping my Slushee and munching my Slim Jims, I sat in silence for a good ten minutes before my dad's warnings rang true and my poor judgment finally caught up with me.

"Mind if I sit here?" said a voice in my left ear, startling me so badly that I almost dropped the last half of my last Slim Jim.

"Uh...n-no," I stammered, the blood draining from my face as the tall, lanky stranger sat down on the bench, two inches away from me, his hands in the pockets of his red and white hoodie, "I... I was just leaving, actually."

"No," he said, grabbing my arm as I tried to get up, "you're stayin' right here with me."

For a moment, my mind flashed back to that day at the lake, then it simply went blank. I realized that I had no clue what to do in that situation. To this day, I am ashamed to say that I have almost no idea what that man even looked like. In my mind, every bad man was the same, and they were all the man that killed my sister, the man who had almost killed me. The man whose gaunt, skeletal face I could never erase from my mind, no matter how hard I tried.

The mugger's claw-like grip on my arm tightened as I squirmed, trying to get out of his grasp but unable to make a single sound.

"Empty your pockets, honey," he said in a sickening, teasing whisper, as if he could seduce me into submission with his arrogant, gravelly voice.

His hand moved from my arm to my thigh and I found my own voice.

"*HELP!*" I screamed, so loud that I swore I could feel my throat tear, "*SOMEBODY HELP ME!!*"

"Shut up!" he ordered gruffly, backhanding me across the face so hard that it knocked me to the ground, where stars flickered in front of my eyes.

But I didn't shut up. I screamed even louder, my voice cracking and breaking as he knelt over me, digging in my pockets and grabbing at my throat, trying to rob me and silence me at the same time.

Finally, one of his hands found my face and he covered my mouth, muffling my voice, my only real defense.

"Just give me the damn money," he panted, glaring down at me, his eyes glinting in the darkness.

I shook my head, trying to get his sweaty hand off of my mouth. I didn't have any money for him to steal—I had spent my last dollar at the gas station just minutes before. I was no fool. I knew what would happen when he didn't find any money in my wallet. I had watched enough *Law and Order: SVU* to know that his hand on my thigh earlier had just been a preview of what was coming.

As I struggled, slapping at him with my useless, flailing arms while my subconscious threatened to transport me back to the other attack I so desperately wanted to forget, my mouth went dry and I realized that there was no way out of the situation. I was being mugged, I would probably be raped, and I was going to die. Whether the thug killed me or not, the person I had been before that moment would be gone forever, and my panicked heart ached as I wondered whether anyone would even miss her.

Just as I began to tell myself that it would all be over soon, that I'd be back with Charlotte, that I'd be free of this cruel, senseless, lonely world forever, a blur of flannel and brown leather came bursting through the darkness, hurling itself at my attacker and tackling him to the ground with a primal roar and a burst of motorcycle exhaust fumes.

For a split second, I just lay on the damp, cold grass, staring up at the broken concrete angel, wondering dazedly if I had somehow slipped into Heaven without noticing my body leaving the Earth.

A loud thud and a sharp yelp brought me back to reality, however, and I sat up just in time to see two bodies rolling toward me, blood and fists flying.

I leapt to my feet and backed up against the two-foot concrete ledge surrounding the fountain's pool. There was another yelp and I saw the mugger break away from the tumbling tornado, his nose clearly broken as he stumbled sideways and fell down again, whining like an injured dog.

But that was not what caught my attention.

"Casey!" I gasped, as my hero pulled himself up from the wet grass, wiping sweat from his brow and blood from his split lip as he towered over his nemesis. As he looked down at his bloody hand, I prayed to God that he wouldn't pass out again.

He didn't.

Growling like a grizzly bear, Casey dropped his hand and bent over to pick the other man up by the collar of his hoodie, dragging him upward and holding him suspended in the air.

"Please don't kill me!" the once-so-tough thug whimpered as his feet dangled two feet off the ground. "That chick is crazy! I wasn't gonna do nothin' to her! Please don't kill me, man!"

"Why shouldn't I?" Casey snarled into his face. Casey's own face was contorted with fiery rage, and I was glad that I was not on the receiving end of his glare.

"Hmy-nuh," the other man squeaked unintelligibly, and I marveled at Casey's ability to transform such a sick, powerful man into a groveling child.

Casey dropped him to the ground dispassionately, apparently satisfied with his answer. He flung him one last withering look of disgust and contempt and walked toward me, limping slightly on his left leg.

"Are you alright?" he asked me. His voice was rough but his

eyes were worried, as if he were praying that he hadn't come too late.

"Y-yeah," I stuttered as he got closer, "but how did--"

Just then, I heard a fevered pounding and I looked away from Casey's bruised face just in time to see the bloody, battered mugger barrel into me, sending both of us flying over the concrete barrier and into the freezing water of the fountain.

Chapter Ten

THE WATER COULDN'T HAVE BEEN MORE than two or three feet deep but I was drowning, I was screaming, I was thrashing as I fought, not the force of the mugger pushing me, but the force of my sister's ghost pulling me down, down, down into the murky depths of the muddy lake in Echols three months and three hundred miles away. The water was freezing and the debris of past fish and fishing trips stung my eyes, but I didn't dare close them. I looked down at Charlotte as she hit the lake floor, her porcelain skin glistening and the bruise around her neck a deep, painful violet in the semi-darkness as she stared at me with her pale, dead eyes.

Dead because of me.

I tried to swim upward, to scream, to cry out for help, but I couldn't. I was bound to Charlotte, by more than just the length of rope Davidson had used to tie our wrists together before throwing us into the water to sink like stones to the lake bottom, where we would both lie forever, dead because of me.

I looked desperately at Charlotte, my only sister, my only friend, my only hope. She just stared back at me with her bulging, unblinking eyes and my waterlogged brain told me to give up, that it was no use; I was already dead.

As the icy water pounded against my ears and obscured my vision, I reached out to gently touch the thick purple bruise on Charlotte's neck. The noose that had hung her was now binding my right wrist to her left, but I wouldn't look at it. I couldn't look at it.

Instead, I watched Charlotte's pretty white sundress as it fluttered in the weak current. My mind grew fuzzy as I recalled that she had borrowed that dress from me, just like she had done a million times before, and just like she should have done a million times after.

I looked once more into her blank, lifeless blue eyes and I whispered, beneath the water, beneath the waves, beneath the living world above, "I'm so sorry, Charlotte."

My mouth filled with water, but I didn't sputter. This was it— my time to die. I had failed Charlotte, and now it was time to accept the consequences.

As a darkness that had nothing to do with the muddy water began to obscure my vision, I looked up toward the surface to get one last glimpse of the sun.

"CLARA!" someone was shouting, but I didn't know who. "CLARA! CAN YOU HEAR ME?"

I shook my head to clear it. I knew how that story ended. No one came to save me. No one pulled me out of the water, and certainly no one screamed my name as if it mattered to them whether or not I lived or died.

"Clara! Hang on!"

I turned away from the sun and closed my eyes. Why wouldn't they just leave me alone? No one could help me, even if they wanted to. I was dead, like Charlotte. There was no saving us.

"*CLARA!* Dammit!"

I opened my eyes to roll them at Charlotte, to share one last inside joke, but she wasn't there. I jerked as I saw that the rope that bound our wrists was gone, and I was alone in the lake.

But it wasn't the lake, was it?

Slowly, the dirty, algae-covered lake bottom was replaced by a solid block of grey cement, and I was terrified.

"Clara!"

I realized that, for the first time, my terror was not due to being alone or dying alone. It was due to the fact that, for the first time in a long time, I wasn't ready to stop living yet. Charlotte was gone, but I didn't have to be. I didn't want to be.

Thrashing sluggishly in the thick, icy water, I turned to look back at the sun, but it was gone too. It had been replaced by an angel. Not a concrete angel, but a real, live, shaggy-haired angel with big, sad brown eyes and a scruffy black beard.

I felt phantom hands grabbing at me, trying to drag me back to the lake in Echols, but I resisted them. I reached toward the angel, who was reaching for me, his hands large and shaky as he grasped me by the forearms and dragged me up, out of the lake, out of the fountain, out of the past.

"Thank God," Casey exhaled as he stood me upright in the water and I sputtered and coughed, hacking the lake out of my lungs. As I choked on the life-giving air, he held one arm around my waist to support me and used his other hand to wipe the hair and water out of my face. "Thank God," he said again, as I accidentally spat water all over his lovely leather jacket.

"I'm...not dead," I wheezed in disbelief as water and who knows what else streamed from my nose.

"No, you're not," Casey said, his voice strangely firm as he gently shook me by the shoulders for some reason, "and you're not going to be anytime soon."

Still confused, I cocked my dizzy head to look up at Casey, who was covered in dirt and blood and worry. Just then, I felt something brush up against my leg and I screamed, scrambling up

Casey's body like a cat, clawing at his shoulders with my hands and using his pants pockets for footholds.

Casey grabbed me tighter and lifted me up over the side of the fountain, and we both looked down to see a dark figure floating on the surface of the rippling water. It was my mugger, alive but unconscious, but for a split second, I saw only the ghost of my sister, drifting slowly across the water and away from me forever. Then it all hit me at once—my sister's death, my mugging, my strange inability to die when Fate kept urging me to—and I threw my arms around Casey's neck, scream-sobbing into his collar as he clutched me to him so tight that it hurt.

"It's okay," he muttered into my freezing, dripping hair as his voice broke. "It's okay, I've got you."

Chapter Eleven

AFTER A QUICK INTERVIEW with the local police force and an even quicker motorcycle ride back to my apartment (during which I rode side sidesaddle in front of Casey with his jacket wrapped around me and my head on his chest), I sat on my kitchen counter, where Casey had deposited me after carrying me across the parking lot and up two flights of stairs to my second-floor walk-up.

"Well, your lip's busted," he told me, holding my face in his rough hands as he squinted at my mouth and I tried to keep my teeth from chattering, "but other than that, you look fine. Which isn't saying much, coming from me."

He grinned, accentuating his own split lip and the rapidly purpling bruise around his left eye. His scruffy face was also covered in a series of other tiny scrapes and bruises, but he didn't seem to mind much, even though just looking at him made me wince.

As he inspected my lower lip more closely, I noticed a thin layer of sweat beginning to bead on his forehead, and I felt slightly guilty. Since I had vehemently protested both showering and going to the hospital, Casey had forced me to let him crank up my furnace to eighty-five degrees so that I wouldn't get hypothermia or pneumonia or some other illness worried mothers always fussed about.

"You can turn the heat down," I said shyly, looking down at my soggy cast and the plastic baggie Casey was making me wear over it until I saw a doctor in the morning.

"Nah," Casey said, bending down so that he could catch my eye, "I'm good."

I tried to smile, but I felt terrible. I was exhausted from almost drowning and from yet again reliving a past I could never change, and I felt awful for causing Casey to get hurt. Most of all, though, I was sickened by my helplessness. I had been helpless to save Charlotte, and I had been helpless to save myself from either my mugger or my own memory. That fountain had not been that deep; I should have been able to stand up and fight. Instead, though, I had almost died from some sort of semi-paralysis brought on by mere remembrances. When had I become so pathetic?

"Hey,'" Casey said, gently placing his thumb and forefinger under my chin and raising my head to make me look at him, "are you okay?"

As I looked into his dark, kind, still-worried eyes, I was suddenly overcome with the urge to tell him everything: how Charlotte had died, how I wasn't always such a coward, and how he was my new personal savior.

Instead, I just said, "Yeah."

Casey sighed and stepped away from the counter. For some strange reason, I had to resist the urge to free my arms from his jacket and pull him back.

"I'm an asshole," he said, leaning his head against the humming refrigerator, his fist clenched at his side.

"No you're n-n-not," I chattered, surprised by his quick change in demeanor. He had obviously misinterpreted my mood and thought that I was angry at him, not at myself.

"Yes I am," he said, turning back around to face me with dark, blazing eyes. "If I hadn't yelled at you for ruining that stupid, little, insignificant piece of blanket—which, by the way, I shouldn't have left in the stinking storeroom in the first place—you would have never ended up in that park!"

"It's n-n-not your f-fault!" I insisted, "I went to that park on my own! And that blanket is not insign-n-n-nificant! It's all you had left of—"

"You could have died!" Casey shouted, "You could have died and it would have been all my fault!"

It is amazing how easily grieving people are able to overlook the obvious facts of an event in order to incriminate themselves. Of course, I was not one to talk.

"Are you kidding me?" I shouted back, my sore throat straining with a fervor it had been missing for quite some time, "Without you, I'd be dead for sure!"

Casey started to speak, but I cut him off.

"I would have been killed by that mugger or I would have drowned in that stupid, shallow fountain!"

In my agitation, I had lost my grip on Casey's leather jacket, and it slipped down my shoulders, exposing my sopping-wet, slightly opaque, green t-shirt. Casey, protective of both my heat and my modesty, came over and pulled it back up, wrapping it more snugly around me, his torso against my knees as he leaned toward the counter.

"Well, I'm still sorry," Casey said softly, stubbornly, brushing a wet curl out of my face and tucking it behind my ear.

"Apology accepted," I replied, just as softly, feeling the now-familiar butterfly wings fluttering faintly against the walls of my tensed stomach. Casey's face was once again only inches from mine, and from that distance, he looked even more attractive than before. His cuts and bruises only made it worse, for they were marks of his devotion to the welfare of a sad, lonesome stranger he had met just a few weeks before.

For a moment, I thought he would kiss me and, for a moment, I wanted him to. But then I realized that I couldn't accept something that intimate from anyone, not yet. It wouldn't be fair. He didn't know what I had done.

But I could tell him.

"I'm afraid of water," I blurted, and I could see from Casey's eyes that I had startled him out of some sort of internal debate. "Every time I so much as turn on a faucet, I freak out. Since my sister died, I've—"

"—been a Goonie," he finished, nodding with faux solemnity.

"A what?" I asked, completely thrown.

"A Goonie," he repeated, a sly grin creeping across his haggard face, "You know, like in that eighties movie. The little Furby-looking things that go crazy when they get wet."

Suddenly I started to laugh. Hard.

"Those are Gremlins!" I giggled, my shivering turning into the shakes of laughter.

"Oh, yeah," he said, turning red but grinning even more broadly.

I laughed a little more, but then I wanted to get down to business.

"Casey, I feel like I owe you the truth about me," I said, trying again to force myself into telling my story, but he shook his shaggy head.

"Not yet," he said, reaching over to put one arm under my legs and one behind my back to hoist me up, off of the counter, and into his arms. It seemed that he was under the impression that I had lost the ability to walk during the mugging, but I wasn't complaining. "I want to hear your story," he continued, not even straining as he carried me into the living room, my legs dangling and dripping all over the ugly beige carpet, "but I don't want you to tell me just because you feel like you owe it to me because of what happened at the park."

"Okay," I shrugged, more than a bit relieved, but also a tiny bit disappointed. "Then I'll just wait."

"Good," he said, plopping down on my battered purple couch

with me on his lap. He pulled over a thick, fuzzy quilt he had found in my hall closet earlier and draped it over the both of us.

I watched, bemused, as he grabbed the remote from the other couch cushion and turned on the television as if he had done it a million times before. He seemed more at home in my apartment than I did. After a quick squabble over what to watch, we settled on a *Tom and Jerry* marathon on the Cartoon Network, and he pitched the remote to the other end of the couch before wrapping both of his arms around my waist over the blanket.

Too tired and too unable to resist his charm, I rested my pounding head on his shoulder and closed my eyes. Each rise and fall of his deep, broad chest reminded me that, unlike most of the company I hosted in my apartment, he was alive.

And so was I.

"Thank you for saving me," I whispered, sleep already washing over me as I inhaled the scent of grass stains and motorcycles from his collar.

"Thank *you* for not dying," he whispered back, his voice slow with weariness but thick with sincerity.

Just as I drifted off into what would turn out to be another rare night of dreamless slumber, I felt the scratch of beard stubble as Casey kissed me on the forehead, then rested his head on top of mine.

Chapter Twelve

I AWOKE at noon the next day, sweating like a menopausal grandmother on a summer afternoon and starving like I hadn't eaten for days. Reluctantly, I disentangled myself from Casey, who grunted, but did not wake. I took a long second to look down at his bruised but placid face as he slept peacefully, his split lips parted and his shaggy head leaning back against the sofa cushion as he emitted a few long, quiet snores.

I grinned.

I had half-expected to wake up and find him gone, but there he was. I was almost giddy with the thought of the scandal and the possibilities that the situation could bring. I, Clara Marie Halpert, notorious geeky introvert and all-around "good girl" had woken up with a man on my couch that morning, and I was planning to keep him there as long as possible.

As quietly as I could, I tiptoed to my bedroom to get some dry clothes. Although it had been at least twelve hours since they had gotten drenched, the clothes I was wearing were still soggy and wrinkled due to the humid sauna Casey had created when he had turned up the thermostat. I changed into some loose jeans and a dirty t-shirt I found on the floor...then I remembered that I had a handsome, heroic guy on my couch and, thus, a rare occasion on which to look my best. I changed into some less-slouchy jeans and a snug-fitting green sweater that highlighted my new, ravioli-fueled curves and appraised myself in the mirror on the inside of my closet door.

For once, I actually looked presentable...aside from my grimy hair and busted lip, the former of which I quickly pulled back into a loose ponytail. Like always, a piece of my long, almost grown-out bangs fell over my left cheek.

As I took myself in, I couldn't help but remember the last time I had looked in the mirror, the day I had broken my hand. Then, just over two weeks ago, I had been gaunt and sickly, lifeless and pale. That day, however, my face, though still pale, was fuller and tinged with a faint blush that I couldn't account for, and there was a strange sort of sparkle in my green eyes that I had never noticed before.

Without really knowing why it was happening, I watched my cracked lips curve upward into a smile.

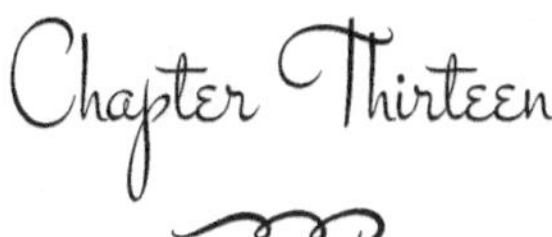

"WHATCHA COOKIN'?" Casey yawned as he stumbled into the kitchen a little while later, running his hand through his already-tousled hair and making it stick up in all directions.

"Ravioli," I answered, feeling almost cheerful as I stirred the pot of bubbling goodness, "food of the gods."

"Awesome," Casey said, yawning again as he took a seat at the table, looking much too large for my tiny kitchen, "Sign me up for some of that."

I chuckled, finding myself unable to think of anything else to say. I was bad enough at conversing without his adorable sleep-ruffledness flustering me! Awkwardly, I turned back to the stove as he tried to rub the sleep out of his eyes.

I turned off the burner as the pasta reached a rolling boil, and Casey let out a low, unexpected "Whoa."

"What?" I frowned, unable to decipher his tone of voice.

"Nothing," he said, shifting uncomfortably in his whitewashed chair. I was even more puzzled as he began to blush, his tan face turning a deep, dark red beneath his greenish-purple bruises and scabby battle scars.

"It looks like something," I said. "Is something wrong?" Then

I gasped, unable to believe the blasphemy I was about to utter. "Do you not like ravioli?"

"Oh no!" he exclaimed, "I mean, yes, I like ravioli—"

I relaxed. Our relationship would never work if I had to choose between him and the Chef.

"—I was just going to say that you look really nice today," he continued, not making eye contact as he blushed a shade darker, "But then I thought, 'Well if I say that, she'll think that I don't think she looks nice every day,' which isn't true, since you looked nice every day at Group, it's just that there's something um, er, different about you today...maybe your sweater? I don't know..." he trailed off, probing a hole in the leg of his blue jeans with his finger. "Smooth move, Linderman," he sighed under his breath.

I felt my own face flush as I fought off another grin. I had never pictured Casey as one to babble, especially after he had been so confident and debonair the night before, but he had just about the sweetest babble I had ever heard. The butterflies were pounding more feverishly than ever against the lining of my empty stomach, and I knew I'd better choose my next words carefully if I didn't want to lose the moment or leave Casey feeling like an idiot.

"Well," I said, getting two bowls out of the cabinet above the sink, as if I hadn't been fazed at all by his endearing display of awkwardness, "You're just not used to seeing me this way. This is actually what I look like on the rare occasions that I'm not panicking, puking, or crying."

Casey's head darted up to see if I was being serious. When he saw that I was, of course, experimenting with my newfound (if somewhat lame) sense of humor, a crooked grin spread across his scruffy face.

After a too-long look that made us both blush even harder, I ladled out the ravioli and placed one bowl in front of him on the polished-oak table and placed the other, slightly fuller, bowl in front of me. As I sat down across from him, Casey let out a moan so loud and so full of ecstasy that I almost felt scandalized.

"Oh my God," he groaned, his eyes rolling back in the pure agony of hot ravioli bliss, "This is the best thing I have ever eaten in my life!"

I snorted into my own pasta.

"That's what I said too," I giggled, watching him shovel two more packets of meaty-cheesy goodness into his already-stuffed cheeks.

Assuming that no one reacts to ravioli like that unless they've been starving themselves for at least a few days, I figured that I had not been the only one missing out on the finer culinary delights of life lately. Out of respect for his pride (and in the interest of being spared any more of his almost-indecent looks of longing toward his lunch), I left him to his meal and focused on eating my own.

After we had both finished, I got a tub of ice cream from the freezer and plopped it down on the table between us.

"I only have two bowls," I explained, somewhat embarrassed, "so we'll both have to eat out of this."

"Sounds good to me," Casey smiled, taking the spoon I offered him.

After a few minutes of quiet eating from me and a few more blissful moans from Casey as he continued his prolonged food-gasm, I felt compelled to ask him something I had been wondering ever since he had pulled me out of the fountain the night before.

"Hey, Casey?" I began casually, studying a drop of melted chocolate as it dripped down the back of my spoon and into the paper carton.

"Mmhmm?"

"How did you know I was in the park last night?"

I glanced up at him and he swallowed hard, looking strangely sheepish.

"Well, to be honest with you..." He sighed, studying his own spoon. "I kind of...well, I followed you."

I wasn't quite sure how to feel about that. Evidently that was apparent in my expression, because Casey hurriedly went on to explain himself.

"I felt terrible about what I said to you in the garage," he said, putting down his spoon and placing his hand on the table, his fingers curled under his palm as if he were resisting the urge to reach out for mine.

Sticking my spoon into the carton of ice cream, I put my free hand on the table too, just in case.

"I was a jerk, and it was my own fault for leaving that blanket in the storeroom in the first place. I wanted to tell you that, and to apologize, and to thank you for patching me up. The minute you walked out that door I regretted everything I'd done, and I knew I had to let you know, so I got on my bike and followed you."

"And you didn't catch up with me until I got to the park?" I asked slowly, an unsettling realization growing ever clearer in my mind. Theoretically, if Casey had wanted to, he could not only have saved me from that mugger, but he could have prevented the entire incident from happening in the first place.

As I felt a surge of indignation and a touch of the anger that had fueled my stride the night before, Casey reached out and grabbed my hand, his skin rough and his palm cold from holding the ice cream box.

"You couldn't have caught me before that guy attacked me?" I continued, unable to even look at him anymore. "You couldn't have given me some sort of warning that he was coming? A heads up would have been nice!"

I regretted putting my hand on the table, and I tried to remove it from his, but he just squeezed it tighter.

"Clara, I'm sorry," he said, sounding pained, "I got to that Thornton's right as you were leaving and I needed to get gas for my bike. I figured you couldn't get that far on foot, so I stopped. I wasn't even there for five minutes, but after that I lost track of you."

He still wouldn't give me my hand back, so I crossed my other arm over my chest.

"When I finally found you again at the park, I thought I was too late," he said, his voice softening as he stroked his thumb across the back of my hand. I looked up at his face and saw a far-off look in his eyes as he clenched his jaw in anger. "When I saw the way that guy was holding you down on the ground, I thought he'd... I thought maybe he had..."

Suddenly he banged his fist on the table, startling me and sending my spoon clattering onto the green linoleum floor. "Clara, I wanted to kill him! I wanted to tear him to pieces! Just the thought of him putting his grimy hands on you, and what he could have done to you—what he almost *did* do to you—made me crazy! It still does."

As my initial anger began to subside, I squeezed his hand, making him meet my eyes once more.

"But weren't you scared?" I asked. I needed to know how he had found the strength to fight off that mugger when I couldn't. If I could only hear how he had done it, maybe I could rediscover a similar strength in myself.

"Hell yeah I was scared!" he exclaimed, "I was scared of getting killed, scared of getting hurt, but mostly I was just scared of losing you before I got the chance to show you that I'm not really the jerk you think I am."

He glanced down at his thick fingers, still interlaced with mine, and looked ashamed.

"I don't think you're a jerk," I said earnestly, already missing his big brown eyes.

"You did last night," he reminded me, trying to take his hand away this time. I wouldn't let him.

"No, I didn't. Not really," I told him, "I just said that because I was mad."

"How could you not have thought that?" he demanded,

sounding a bit bitter, "I mean, I kicked a freaking drill at you, for crying out loud! What did you think I was, if not a jerk?"

I was quiet for a moment. Then he looked up at me with his sad, haunted eyes and against my better judgment, I felt closer to him then than I had felt to anyone in a long, long time.

"I thought you were hurting," I answered quietly, looking down at our hands, "just like me."

Chapter Fourteen

Four hours later, I was feeling more physical than emotional pain as we sat across from each other in a booth at a McDonald's not far from the hospital. A very judgmental doctor had reset my hand and recast my cast, all the while scolding me for being so reckless and "flippant" with the first one. After fifteen minutes of trying to explain myself, I had tuned him out and had chosen to focus instead on the way that Casey's dry, tanned fingers looked between mine as he sat beside me on the exam table, holding my hand and urging me to "squeeze it whenever it hurt." Although it hurt like a bitch, I had refrained from too much squeezing—I didn't want to damage his hand in case I wanted to hold it again later.

"Ugh," I groaned, setting down the last half of my second double cheeseburger on its waxy paper wrapper, "I shouldn't have refused those pain meds they offered me."

My hand was throbbing along with every beat of my heart, and every now and then a jolt of pain would shock me nearly to tears. In my still-too-fragile emotional state, however, I had been a bit afraid of what I could do with a bottle of pain killers and no adult supervision. Consequently, I was tired, I was sore, and I just wanted to go home. What I didn't want, though, was to lose my chance to spend time with the only person I had actually felt like spending time with in what felt like an eternity.

"Still hurts, huh?" Casey asked, grimacing in sympathy before starting in on his third Big Mac.

I gave him a miserable nod and put my head down on the dirty table, on top of my good arm.

"Do you want me to take you home?"

"No!" I said quickly, my voice muffled by my jacket sleeve. As much as I enjoyed sitting so close behind him that I could feel him breathe, Casey's motorcycle had jostled my arm so badly on the way to and from the hospital that I was dreading ever getting back astride that magnificent, gas-powered stallion again.

"Well, on the bright side, your cast looks really cool."

I squinted up at him to see if he was serious. I couldn't tell.

"Really?" I asked, dubious, as I scowled at the busboy clearing the table behind Casey.

"Yeah," he smiled, "Who else would pick a neon-orange cast?"

Although my first cast had been orange against my wishes, I had grown quite fond of the color over the few short weeks it had been a part of my ensemble.

"It reminds me of a painting I did once," I told him, looking down at the carefully wrapped strips of plaster with affection and an odd, pleasant sort of nostalgia. "It was of a sunset, and it took me forever to get the color just right. But when I did, it was just...perfect."

"You're an artist?" Casey asked, his head tilted to the side, as if he were studying me.

I froze. For a moment, I had forgotten that I hadn't known Casey all my life, and that he hadn't known the person that I was before I lost Charlotte, the person that I was so rapidly forgetting with each miserable day that passed.

"I *was* an artist," I said slowly, feeling somewhat guilty for having forgotten to think about Charlotte long enough to recall a pleasant memory that didn't involve her.

Casey didn't ask me anything else about it, for which I was grateful. I had loved painting; it had once been as important to me as breathing or eating. Imagination and creativity are quick to fade, however, when all of your mental processes are focused on guilt, grief, and anxiety. It is especially difficult to be an artist when that choice is a large part of what brought about your sister's death.

"I'm gonna go get some more fries," Casey said a while later, as I poked listlessly at my now-tepid burger with my finger.

When he stood up, something fell from his pocket. I was on the verge of opening my mouth to call out to him, but then I saw what had fallen.

Rosie's blanket.

Battered, blood-stained, and faded, that small square of fabric held the key to unlocking the mystery of Casey's past, but it also bore the marks of my present shame. I glanced up at Casey, who was at the counter ordering from the tiny Vietnamese woman who had severed us earlier. Then, I did something I hoped I wouldn't regret later.

I slid to the edge of the sticky, plastic, couch-like seat and leaned over, snatching the swatch from the floor and shoving it into the pocket of my blue jeans before anyone noticed a thing. I had no clue what I was going to do with it but, for whatever reason, I knew that I needed to take it.

Casey came back a few minutes later with a large carton of steaming fries and an even larger grin.

"What?" I asked suspiciously, trying not to look like someone who had just stolen someone else's most prized possession.

"I figured out what your arm needs," he answered, shoving nine or ten fries into his mouth at once while he reached into his jacket pocket.

I held my breath, hoping he wasn't about to realize what he was missing.

Then, to my complete bewilderment, he pulled out a thin, black marker.

"My arm needs a Sharpie?" I asked, not following as he held out his left hand, gesturing for me to hand over my cast.

"No," he replied, his grin broadening at my confusion, "It needs signatures. Every cast needs signatures."

I laughed, feeling both stupid and relieved. "Go for it," I said, shrugging good-naturedly as I proffered my cast.

He frowned, holding the marker cap between his teeth as he turned my hand over, trying to find the perfect spot to put his John Hancock.

"I always wanted a cast when I was a kid," he said, deciding to write sideways on the inside of my palm. "I thought it would make me look like a bad-ass."

"Does it make *me* look like a bad-ass?" I asked, pilfering a few of his fries while he wrote.

"Hell yeah," he replied, finishing his signature with a grand and unnecessary flourish. "How'd you get this anyway?"

"I punched a wall," I said, feeling a little sheepish. What had seemed like a horrible and shameful act a few days ago now just seemed silly.

"Wow," he replied, putting the cap back on the marker. If he was shocked or judgmental, he didn't let it show. "I'd ask you why you did it, but I don't want to piss off a chick that goes around punching walls."

I stuck my tongue out at him, something I hadn't done since I was twelve. Then I looked down at my cast to see what he had written in the same untidy, yet still-legible, scrawl that embellished the sign above Linderman's Garage.

"To my favorite Goonie," it read, "Feel better soon. Your friend, Casey Linderman."

"The movie's called *Gremlins*," I reminded him, laughing. I had thought he was just going to write his name, but instead he had written an unexpectedly sweet message with two of the best words I had ever seen together: "Your friend."

"Oh yeah," he said, smacking his forehead with his huge palm, "Here, let me fix it."

"No!" I objected, pulling my cast into my chest to shield it from him. "I like it better this way."

"Fine," he said, smiling his crooked smile, "have it your way. Now everyone else who signs it will get to see what an idiot I am."

"That's not going to be a problem," I said, losing a bit of my good humor. "You're the only person I know who would sign it."

Casey stared at me for a moment, looking thoughtful as he munched on his rapidly-cooling fries. I shifted my glance to the tabletop, feeling self-conscious, as if I had once again revealed too much.

"Give me your cast back," he said decisively, reaching out for my hand.

"What are you gonna do?"

"Just let me see it for a second," he insisted, wriggling his fingers impatiently.

Reluctantly, I gave in and put my aching hand in his.

"Now look over there," he instructed, pointing out the window behind me at a bunch of kids playing on the McDonald's Playplace outside.

"What—"

"Clara, please?"

He gave me the saddest set of big, brown puppy-dog eyes I had ever seen, and I, of course, did as he asked and turned with a sigh to look out the window. Casey then proceeded to scratch at my cast again as I tried not to wince. I watched a little boy fall off the monkey bars twice, a girl spit on a baby three times, and another one throw up on the slide before Casey finally said, "There! You can look now."

Not sure what I would see when I looked down, I brought my hand over and placed it on the table in front of me.

"Read it," Casey encouraged.

There, in the middle of my palm, was his original message, but that was no longer the only thing decorating the hard, uneven surface of the plaster. Now, the entire thing was covered in signatures, all differing in shape, size, and style, and all bearing varied versions of the same name: Casey Linderman.

There must have been at least fifty of them. There were some that just said "Casey," others that said "Mr. Linderman," and even some that read "Casey Charles Linderman." Some were in cursive, some were in print; some were bold, some were thin, some were crammed together, some were spread apart; some were tiny, some were in big black, blocky letters, but each and every one of them spawned a dozen butterflies in my stomach and contributed to one very large lump in my throat.

"Everybody deserves a cast full of signatures," Casey said quietly, shrugging as he watched my reaction.

"Thank you," I whispered, so touched that I was barely able to choke out the words that could not even begin to describe how much such a simple gesture had meant to me.

"Plus," he added with a sly look as I wiped the corners of my eyes, "now you'll never be able to forget my name."

"Trust me," I said thickly, "you don't have to worry about that."

Chapter Fifteen

THAT EVENING, after a quick ravioli-run and another excruciatingly bumpy motorcycle ride, Casey dropped me off at my apartment, vowing to return the next day at lunchtime to help me "throw back a few more cans of Chef Boyardee." I waved as he drove away, and I didn't stop until he had been out of sight for several minutes.

Sighing, I leaned my head against the doorjamb and stared out into the early-evening twilight. Although I'd only spent about twenty-four full hours with Casey and he'd only been gone for a few minutes, I missed him already. My hand was still throbbing, but something else, something in my chest, ached with an equally painful, melancholy throb as I thought about his crooked smile, his deep, throaty chuckle, and the way he had wrapped his large, protective arms around me the night before, making me feel small and safe and cared-for.

Shutting the door behind me, I walked over and plopped down on the sofa with another heavy sigh, followed by a grunt of pain as I landed on my aching arm. As I stretched out my still-faintly-rumbling legs and rested my cast atop my flutter-less stom-ach, I swore I could still feel the scratch of Casey's itchy whiskers on my forehead. In an attempt to distract myself from my adolescent pining, I took Casey/Rosie's blanket/rag out of my pocket and held it up in front of my face.

As I had expected, it was much worse for wear than it would have been if I had never come into contact with it. I recalled Casey's bruises and scrapes and wondered darkly if the same applied to him.

With a strange mixture of guilt for stealing it and an overwhelming reverence for the meaning it held, I slowly ran my finger across the soft, matted fabric. All at once, I could picture it, not as a scrap of soiled garbage, but as a child's cozy, lovable security blanket. I could imagine a little girl with Casey's dark hair and mysterious brown eyes snuggling with it as she sat on her big brother's lap, laughing.

I bolted upright, nearly dropping the blanket scrap.

What had I done?

I had stolen Casey's only real, tangible tie to his dead baby sister, and for what? Curiosity? Shame? Some sort of sick brand of jealousy?

Then it hit me; the reason I had stolen the blanket, the reason I had hidden it. I wasn't supposed to keep it, I was supposed to fix it! I had to atone for my mistake, I had to fix what I had broken. I had to prove that I was worthy to be Casey's friend. No matter how badly I wanted to, I couldn't make up for what I had done to Charlotte, but I could do it for Casey.

Brimming with a sense of purpose like I had never felt before, I leapt off the couch and into the kitchen, where I turned on the faucet, forgetting, for the moment, to be afraid of the cold, rushing water. As I stoppered the sink and watched the silver basin fill up with now-steaming water, however, memories of Charlotte and the lake brushed against me like the needy, grabbing hands of a spoiled child begging for his mother's attention.

I brushed them off.

I had no time for reminiscing. After three and a half useless, sedentary months, it was finally time for action.

As the water level rose, I added some dish soap and activated it with the sprayer nozzle, causing a flood of white, foamy bubbles to fill the sink and begin to cascade downward, over the side of the counter. I turned off the faucet and took one long, last look and the soiled sheet before plunging it into the depths of the water that I had been so afraid to enter myself.

For ten minutes I scrubbed, I scrunched, I kneaded that rag until the bubbles were gone and the sink ran red.

But it wasn't enough.

After all that scrubbing, after all that I had risked to rectify my stupid mistake, my efforts were for naught. The pink and purple blanket, now soggy and swollen, was still blood-soaked, still stained, still ruined.

I gave it one more rinse in some clean water before I wrung it out and laid it on the kitchen table. I spread it out flat so that it could dry enough for me to shamefacedly return it to Casey the next day, and so that I could sit down in a chair and stare at it morosely for a little while longer.

It wasn't hard to see how a little girl could have loved a blanket like that. It was cottony and soft, and the little pink bunnies that danced across the deep purple backdrop were so cheery and jovial that they almost brought a smile to even my perpetually pouting lips.

I bit my bottom lip, frowning in concentration as I tried to think of some way to make up for my now doubly heinous crime. Should I lie to Casey and tell him that I had found the blanket on the floor and had just forgotten to give it back to him earlier? Or should I tell the truth and confess that I had willfully stolen the swatch for reasons that hadn't even been clear to me at the time?

Neither option seemed appealing. I couldn't lie to Casey after all he had done for me, but I couldn't tell him the truth either. I didn't want to do anything to change his opinion of me, and I didn't want him to look at me the way he had in the garage the night before, with a look so full of hurt and anger that I winced just thinking about it. I had to find another way to make it up to him. He obviously cared about that blanket, and I obviously cared about him.

With the rusty wheels of invention turning slowly in my head, I stood up and paced toward my bedroom. Maybe, by some magical stroke of good fortune, I had a blanket that resembled Rosie's. Or, better yet, maybe I still had one of Charlotte's tight, cleavage-bearing tops that would make Casey forget about the blanket all together.

Clambering over several open, disheveled, cardboard moving boxes, I crossed my all-but-abandoned room and opened the door to the tiny closet. I had not slept in the bedroom since I had moved into the apartment. Instead, I had been using it as a large storage unit, mainly to hold all of the things I either didn't want or didn't want to think about. There were boxes of clothes, boxes of books, boxes of school papers and boxes of things that weren't even mine, and I didn't want to look at any of it. My mother had forced me to take it all with me when I moved out, but she couldn't force me to open the boxes and look inside, let alone take out the contents and give them a permanent place in my eerie, already-haunted apartment.

Inside the three-foot wide closet in which I had hidden the things I was even more anxious to forget about, I shoved aside a few more boxes full of Charlotte's old clothes before I could get caught up in painful memories again. Ignoring the sleeve of her favorite cardigan as it waved at me from its cardboard coffin, I found the box I was looking for.

My breath quickened and I began to grow panicked as Charlotte's memories threatened to overtake me again. Her presence was like a fog slowly rising up out of the carpet and wrapping itself around my neck like a thick woolen scarf, threatening to choke me. Suddenly I could see Charlotte laughing as we put on mini-fashion shows for each other before school every single morning for sixteen years, exchanging clothes and compliments as if we were not only sisters, but best friends.

I shook my head firmly.

I had a new friend now, and he needed me to shove Charlotte back in the closet for the moment and repair what I had ruined.

I threw open a box labeled "GIRLS' BED STUFF" and began rummaging within it for something, anything, that resembled pink bunnies. A rainbow, tie-died quilt? No. A baby-blue down comforter? Nope. A twin sheet set covered with dancing frogs? Close, but no cigar. I threw the rejected blankets onto the floor, my movements getting faster and wilder as I grew more and more hopeless.

Then I found it.

There, at the bottom of the box lay the answer I had been searching for. There, atop the warped cardboard and amidst the clumps of dryer lint was a thin, frayed, royal purple blanket and something I never thought I would see again.

My art supplies.

All my life, I had wanted to be an artist. In kindergarten, I was painting portraits of Elmo and Oscar the Grouch, and by middle school I was painting landscapes of the cafeteria and my backyard. By the time I had gotten to college, I had not only moved on to more sophisticated subjects, but had realized that painting was my passion, my life's work, the key to my future happiness. I had lost days, even weeks, at a time painting people from memory or landscapes from my bedroom window. Every little ladybug, every imperceptible crease in a tree trunk had inspired me to paint, and soon painting was an even bigger part of my life than even Charlotte was. When I was painting, it was as if I had entered another world where the ideas just flowed through me, as if I were some sort of conduit to someone else's vision. It had been wonderful, it had been beautiful, and it had made me happier than anything else I had ever done, or would ever do again.

I began to reach for the scratched, faded, paint-covered tackle box that had once been as much a part of me as my own right hand, but then I stopped. My fingers began to tremble. Could I really do this? After all this time, could I open the door that I had closed so long ago to protect not only myself, but everyone I loved from getting hurt the way Charlotte did?

As I knelt there on the floor, irresolute, my unsteady hand outstretched toward the past I had nearly forgotten and the future that could once have been mine, I recalled a day in late spring when Charlotte had come to visit me in my art class.

"So, where's this amazing sunset portrait I've heard so much about?" she had asked, sweeping into the room like a warm summer breeze and causing every male in the room (straight or otherwise) to drop whatever they were doing and stare, unabashedly, at her long, tanned legs and her snug-fitting, daisy-yellow, spaghetti-strap sundress.

Wherever Charlotte went, she had always been the center of attention. She was beautiful by any standard that you could measure her by; a strange mixture of a goddess and the girl-next-door, she was stunning but not intimidating, gorgeous without knowing why, and sexy, but with a kindness that made everyone, man or woman, wonder which was sweeter: her body or her disposition.

Charlotte, being used to the attention of ogling strangers by that point, threw the boys a bone and gave them one of her most sparkly, knock-out smiles and a flirtatious flip of her long, wavy, blonde hair to tide them over until she returned to them that night in their dreams.

"It's not a portrait, Char," I scolded her, giving the men in the room a withering look. "Portraits are of people."

"Oh, duh," she said, slapping a perfectly manicured hand against her forehead. I glanced down at my own thin, pale, grubby-looking hand covered in paint-spatter, but she interrupted my brief burst of sisterly jealousy by grabbing it. "Come on!" she urged, "I really want to see your painting!"

And the thing was, she really did.

Charlotte had always been my biggest fan, and she had more of my paintings in her closet or on her walls than I did. She would even go through my trash to "rescue" the unfinished paintings I had thrown out. When I had told her that they were no good, she would always say the same thing: "They're good enough for me!" Charlotte may have been eyed by every man she met, but when she and I were together, she only had eyes for me... well, unless a particularly hot guy hit on her, of course.

"Follow me," I told her, pulling her by the hand over to the back corner of the gigantic, warehouse-like art classroom.

We must have made quite a pair: she with her beauty and irresistible charm, and me with my out-of-style, paint-speckled clothes and near-crippling shyness. But that didn't matter. Charlotte was two and a half years older than me, but we may as well have been twins. There was not one thing we didn't share; from clothes and secrets and bedrooms to colds and flus and food poisoning. My parents had said that Charlotte and I were like one person living in two bodies, an idea that we had embraced with enthusiasm from the time we were in diapers.

"Ooooo, is that it?" Charlotte gasped as we reached the back of the cavernous, unfinished brick-walled room.

"Yep," I said, grinning proudly as I stood in front of my latest masterpiece. "What do you think?"

"Oh, Clara, it's beautiful," she marveled, her voice almost a whisper as her awe-filled blue eyes took in the deep, almost neon-orange of the sun and the meticulously mixed pinks and purples of the clouds in my "portrait" of a sunset. "I think it's the best one you've ever done!"

"It ought to be," came the cool, confident voice of my art professor from over our shoulders. "She's been working on this thing for six weeks now."

I blushed and started to stammer something not even I could have understood, so Charlotte took over, grabbing the conversational reins with such ease and grace that I wondered how we could be related.

"You must be Professor Davidson," Charlotte guessed, giving him a dazzling smile as she extended her hand to shake his.

"You can call me David," he replied warmly, his smile lighting up his gaunt, chiseled features as he shook her hand for much too long.

"David Davidson?" Charlotte said, with a tinkling laugh that stopped my continuous blushing and unintelligible stammering instantly.

She was flirting with him.

At only thirty-one, Davidson was young for a professor, and despite his pallid, vampirish skin, he was quite good-looking. His grey eyes sparkled from atop sharp, well-pronounced cheekbones and his brown, purposely unkempt hair made him seem more relatable than any other professor I had ever had. Plus, he was an artistic genius; his paintings of dismembered mannequins, though dark and creepy, were exquisite. So exquisite, in fact, that several of them were hanging in a nearby museum as we spoke.

I could see why Charlotte would be attracted to him; she had always been big on the artsy, handsome, hippie-types, but there was something about him that had always seemed off to me. It was as if there were something dark and terrible lurking behind his granite eyes and within his gruesome paintings of agony and despair. Up until that point, however, I had dismissed the dement- edness of his work as an expression of his creativity, an exercise in connecting to the darkness that lies within us all. But as he stood there, still shaking my sister's hand, I knew in my gut that their relationship would be the beginning of some sort of end. I knew, somehow, that his involvement in our lives would only bring disaster.

I only wish I would have had the courage to act on that knowl- edge sooner.

Chapter Sixteen

AN HOUR after I found my art supplies, I was lost in a world I had been missing for far too long. I had spread the thin, purple cotton blanket out over the scuffed linoleum floor in my tiny kitchen, having first pushed and shoved my tiny table and my tiny chairs out into the tiny hallway. I had come to terms with the fact that I could not salvage the scrap from Rosie Linderman's blanket. No matter what I did, I could not restore it to its former glory, at least not with any of the materials I had on hand. But I was not yet ready to admit defeat. I was determined to repair the damage I had done and, if I was lucky, I might even be able to rekindle the spark of artistic creativity in my soul that had, until that moment, been reduced to a pile of barely smoldering ashes.

As much as I had been thinking about Casey before I started on it, I dipped my trusty old one-inch flat brush into the small, sticky pot of semi-dried "Salmon Blush" paint and that project became all about me. My already-overworked left hand was gripped tight and close to the bristles as I carefully, tediously sculpted the first six-inch tall bunny. Its long, floppy ears streamed behind it as it leapt over an imaginary stream toward the second bunny, which was dancing in place, its button nose turned up toward the sky and its big, goofy back feet mimicking a ballerina on pointe. Beside that one, I painted a rabbit who was sleeping (most likely tired from all of the leaping and the dancing), and two more who were kissing, their tiny little noses just touching. Another bunny hid its face behind its furry paws, as if playing hide-and-seek, and one was just sitting there, smiling as it took in all of the other action.

It was not the most interesting piece I had ever painted, not by a long shot, and it was not going to be the best, but it was already one of my favorites. No matter what I said and no matter what Casey thought, I would always see that blanket as a new beginning; a rebirth of my dreams of being an artist. As paint splattered against my arms and sweat beaded on my paint-smeared forehead from ignoring the persistent ache in my stiff left hand, I made a promise to myself that it would not be my last piece. The joy of self-expression through art was like a drug for me, and I couldn't see how I had gone without a fix for so long. My mind, always foggy with grief and pain, was becoming clearer with every brush stroke. Colors were brighter: the pink bunnies seemed to glow with the light from the ceiling fan fixture above me, and the purple of the blanket itself had turned into something much richer, much darker, much more meaningful. I had left the world of melancholy and self-pity behind me and had entered a much smaller world, a much better world, where there was only me and my art, and where everything was beautiful and everything made sense.

Hour after hour passed and pot after pot of tempera paint emptied itself until finally, at eight o'clock the next morning, it was finished.

Exhausted but exuberant, I pitched my paintbrush into the sink and stood up, shaking the cramp out of my hand as I took in my masterpiece of mixed-media art. Twenty-seven pink rabbits covered the plum-colored sheet, and looked almost identical to the ones on Rosie's swatch, which I had safety-pinned to the middle of my blanket (I was a painter, not a seamstress). I could not believe that I had been able to paint so well and with such finesse with my left hand.

"Less-dominant hand, my ass," I scoffed, feeling a bit giddy.

The blanket was perfect. Each pink bunny had a different pose, and each one looked as if they had been screen-printed onto the fabric instead of painted by my clumsy, ever-trembling left hand. I smiled with a rare sense of pride, and decided to leave the bunnies to dry in peace while I went to go clean up before Casey came over.

After taking a short but mercifully uneventful shower, I got dressed in one of my old, paint-covered black t-shirts and a pair of cute, paint-speckled jeans and curled up on the couch, feeling more like myself than I had in ages. As I drifted off to sleep, I couldn't help but smile as I imagined what Casey's reaction to my gift would be.

Chapter Seventeen

But Casey never showed up.

I spent hours waiting for him to burst through the unlocked door with his charming, crooked smile and an easily-acceptable excuse for being late, but he never did.

Instead, I ate lunch alone.

I ate dinner alone.

I watched television alone.

And at midnight, twelve hours after he was supposed to arrive, I crumpled up the stupid, ridiculous, childish bunny blanket and threw it in my room before sitting down on my living room couch to cry. Alone.

Chapter Eighteen

That night, as I lay, fully clothed, beneath a quilt on my living room couch, I was too emotionally drained to fight off the memories that I had been getting so much better at repressing when I was with Casey. While I had been lonely before, the loneliness after Casey was more intense somehow, as if by befriending him I had allowed myself to become even more vulnerable than I already was.

I tossed and turned as Charlotte's face swam before me, her eyes blank and her porcelain skin cold. As I watched, balanced precariously on the edge of sleep and wakefulness, her eyes slowly filled with life, but not with love, as suddenly we were back in our old room, the cheerful white daisies on the bright yellow wallpaper mocking us as we screamed at each other.

"Why won't you just let me be happy, Clara?" Charlotte had shouted, her blue eyes blazing as her blonde ringlets fell from her ponytail and into her red, furious face.

"I'm not saying you can't be happy, Char!" I shouted back, brushing my own curls out of my face as we stood, glaring at each other, from across the room. "I'm just saying that Professor Davidson isn't the right guy for you!"

"His name is David," she spat, "and you don't know anything about what's 'right' for me. You don't know me at all!"

I recoiled as if she had slapped me, my anger disappearing as it was replaced by the pain of a betrayal I had never felt before.

"How can you say that?" I asked, my voice falling from a shout to a near whisper.

"You're a kid, Clara," Charlotte said haughtily, snatching up her purse and pulling on her cheap, plastic, daisy-encrusted flip-flops that matched the pretty white sundress she was wearing. *My pretty white sundress.* "You may know about painting and portraits and perspectives and all that, but you know nothing about love, especially not the love between David and me."

"Love?" I repeated incredulously, *"LOVE?!* You've been only been dating for a few weeks, Charlotte! You don't love him."

"You're just jealous," Charlotte deflected, reaching for the shiny silver doorknob that would let her escape her room, her argument, and her stupid, naive little sister.

"Jealous?!"

"Yeah!" she bellowed, turning on her heel to stride across the room, putting her face three inches from mine as she said, with a fury in her eyes I had never seen, "You wanted David for yourself! You've had a crush on him for years; he told me! And I've seen the way you look at his paintings! Sorry, little sister, but you missed your chance. He's mine now, and there's nothing you can do about it."

"You're wrong," I said, backing away from her with tears in my eyes. I had never wanted Davidson; I had feared him! There was so much darkness in his paintings that he could no longer explain away with his clever philosophizing and symbolism, and in recent weeks he had become so cagey and withdrawn in class that he could barely teach the course at all. "Please don't go out with him again, Charlotte," I begged, dropping all pretense and grabbing her hand.

Her sneer faltered and, for a moment, she was my sister again.

But then, just like that, she was gone.

"I will do what I want," Charlotte said firmly, ripping her hand from mine as she stormed out of the room, my sundress billowing behind her.

As she slammed the door, I sat down on the edge of my bed and put my face into my paint-speckled hands.

I rolled over on the couch, teetering dangerously between consciousness and unconsciousness, between the past and the present, between reality and unreality.

The water began to wash over me.

Charlotte's dead face floated before me, her wrist bound tight to mine. I thrashed and struggled, but it was no use. I turned to take one last look at Charlotte, but she was gone. Her ghoulish face had been replaced by a large, dark, strangely demented one.

Casey's.

His brown eyes bulged as he writhed in the water and I sank like a stone, pulling him down with me. His mouth opened into a silent scream and he inhaled a mouthful of water. He coughed and sputtered and I tried to reach out to him, but my vision was obscured as the water changed to thick, sticky, viscous blood.

I screamed as I inhaled the coppery taste of certain death. I could barely see Casey as he pointed down at our wrists, tied together by Charlotte's noose, and it was there that I found the source of all the blood.

There, at the bottom of the lake, Casey's wrist was oozing blood like a sunken tanker leaking oil.

Chapter Nineteen

I JERKED AWAKE, gasping for air and sobbing so hard that I could barely stand up and stumble into the kitchen to search for the phonebook that had come free with the apartment. I found it tucked behind some expired spaghetti sauce in a kitchen cabinet and crashed down onto the floor with it, my chest heaving and my throat tight.

I had to find his number. I had to call him and make sure that he was alright. Why had I automatically jumped to the conclusion that he'd abandoned me? Maybe he was hurt, lying in a parking lot somewhere bleeding while I sat in my apartment trying to force myself to either hate him or forget about him!

In my desperation, I turned the thin, yellow pages so hard and so fast that several of them ripped right out of the book and fluttered faintly in the air like snow before falling softly onto the cold, cracked linoleum floor.

Limpert, Linch, Lind, Linda.

"Come on," I groaned, scanning the tiny print on the page with blurry eyes as my tears smudged the ancient ink.

Lindenschmidt, Linder...Linder...

Linders.

I threw the book across the kitchen and buried my face in my arms. Why was the garage's number unlisted? Why hadn't I asked for Casey's phone number before he left?

Why hadn't he shown up?

I sobbed into my shirt sleeves, despising Casey for what he had done to me, what he had turned me into. Before I had met him, I had been depressed, yes. I had been lonely, sure. But I had never been afraid like I was at that moment; afraid of losing someone else I cared about, afraid of losing myself, afraid of losing my mind. I had just met him; I should not have had such intense feelings for him.

But I did.

As I tried to stop envisioning his terrified, bulging eyes and gushing wrist cut, there was a knock at my door.

Startled, I wiped my nose on my collar and stood up, checking the clock on the stove.

3:47 a.m.

I hesitated. Who could be at my door at that hour?

I wiped my cheeks on the back of my shaking, ink-stained hand as the knock came again, this time harder, louder, more urgent.

Biting my lip in indecision, I took a step closer to the door, just as the visitor knocked once more.

"Clara!" he croaked, his voice strangled and scared.

My stomach dropped.

"Casey?" I whispered, knowing full well that he could not possibly have heard me.

"Clara, answer the door," the voice begged me, "Please!"

I crept to the door and stood on my tiptoes to look out the peephole. There, with his head against my doorjamb and his fists balled at his sides, stood Casey, the one person who could simultaneously save my life and ruin it.

Before he could knock again, I opened the door and glared at him, tears still rolling down my burning cheeks.

"Hey," he started, his red-rimmed, bloodshot eyes lighting up. Seeing the look on my face, however, he faltered. "Clara, what—"

Then I punched him in the stomach.

"How could you do this to me?!" I screamed, shaking my aching left hand. He didn't even have the decency to pretend like my punch had hurt him, even though I was about sixty percent sure I had just shattered my last good hand on his concrete abdominal muscles. He did, however, grant me the satisfaction of looking scared.

"I waited for you all day!" I continued, sniffling and sobbing, my voice breaking more and more as I got louder and louder, "I thought something had happened to you!" I felt my rage ebb as I flashed back to the dream I had just had, to Charlotte's dead face, to Casey's. "I...I thought you might be..."

I trailed off, my voice quiet as the anger left me, only to be replaced by what felt like a swirling, fiery tornado of fear and humiliation. I had overreacted. Casey was not dead, but now he knew how I felt about him; how I felt after just a few weeks. I should have learned from Charlotte's mistake. It was too soon to care that much for someone. It was much too soon.

Wiping my eyes, I turned back to my living room, my shoulders still shaking with unshed sobs as I crossed my arms and tried to regain control of myself and my emotions.

"What are you doing here, anyway?" I asked tremulously.

For a moment, a tense, heavy silence filled the space between us. Then he spoke.

"It was Rosie's birthday today," he said slowly, uncertainly. I could feel the rumble of his low timbre in my aching chest. "I had almost forgotten about it, since I had been spending so much time either with you or thinking about you."

"I'm sorry," I said stiffly, not knowing what he wanted me to say, and not yet ready to face him and try to decipher his emotions when I could barely keep up with my own.

"No, don't be," he replied, brushing my arm as he edged past to stand in front of me so that I would have to look at him. "I'm the one who should be sorry. I should have been here earlier, or I should have called." His eyes fell to his hands, which were stained with blood once more. My heart leapt to my throat. "Most of all, though," he continued, "I shouldn't have been alone."

Slowly, he used one trembling, blood-caked hand to pull up his left shirt sleeve to reveal another, much smaller slice on his wrist, just centimeters above the one I had bandaged before.

I had to resist the urge to reach out and take his hand.

"You're the only person that knows about this," he told me, rolling up his sleeves to bare both arms.

I gasped. His left arm was covered in thin, straight, slightly raised scars, like dozens of tiny cat-scratches all over his skin. I reached out a wet, shaking finger to touch one, to share in his pain, but before I could, Casey took my hand.

"I don't know how or why," he said quickly, as if he were trying to say it before he lost his nerve, "but something's happened to me. To us. Before I met you, I was a mess—an even bigger mess than I am now, believe it or not. But the minute I saw you, something changed."

Casey stopped to gather his courage and his words as I waited, staring into his beautifully haunted brown eyes and listening to the rapid pounding of my own heart. "Clara, when I'm with you, I'm...better. I don't think about my dad as much, or the garage, or Rosie. I just think about how I felt when you first smiled at me in Group or the way your tiny little hand fits so perfectly in mine, or the way you looked at the garage the other day, like it was something special; like you could see the potential in it where no one else could. That's the same way you look at me. No one has ever looked at me like that before," he whispered, running his thumb across the back of my hand as my breath caught in my throat. "I've been thinking about it all night, and it makes no sense since we just met and all, but I...I'm a different person when I'm with you. And I like that person a hell of a lot better than the person I usually am.

In fact," I was a bit startled to hear his voice crack. He gave a self-conscious chuckle and continued, "right now I'm kind of terrified of the person I am when I'm not with you."

I took my hand from his and gently placed it on his right cheek, grazing his stubbly chin as he leaned his face into my palm.

"I'm kind of sorry I punched you now," I sniffled sheepishly. His earnestness had caught me off guard, resurrecting the butterflies in my stomach and an almost-painful fluttering in my heart.

Casey's eyes were filled with tenderness and some deeper, unspoken sentiment as he looked down at me.

"Just kind of?" he teased, his deep voice soft and affectionate.

As I gave a hiccupping laugh, he leaned down to put his arms around my waist, pulling me into a snug embrace. I, in turn, wrapped my arms around his neck and, standing on my tiptoes, I whispered in his ear, "I'm so glad you came back."

Chapter Twenty

"CLARA, I think I should tell you about Rosie."

My fingers fumbled over the gauze I was wrapping around Casey's wrist as he sat atop the toilet in my bathroom, his sleeves rolled up and his flannel shirt unbuttoned to expose his wife-beater-style tank and the tense, taut muscles of his stomach.

"Are you sure?" I asked hesitantly, not at all sure that I was ready to hear it.

"I'm sure," he replied, though the pained expression on his face made me doubt it. "If we ever want whatever *this*—" he gestured to him and to me and then back again "—is to work, I have to be honest with you. I have to tell you everything."

I pretended to check the tape on his gauze as I took a moment to deal with the facts that: a) he wanted us to have a deeper relationship, b) he was getting ready to tell me his deepest, darkest secret, and c) that that meant that I would have to eventually tell him mine too.

"Okay," I sighed, my throat dry. "Um, why don't we go in the living room, where it's more comfortable?"

Casey nodded wordlessly, his pale face tinged with green and his thin lips pressed together, as if he were struggling not to vomit.

"Or we could just stay in here," I added hastily. Vomit is much easier to clean off of a tile floor than a carpeted one.

He nodded again, and I sat down on the raised edge of the shower stall. My legs tingled as our knees touched, but he didn't shift away.

"Uh…" he mumbled, looking strangely ashamed and embarrassed as he ran a hand through his hair, "I don't really know where to start."

"Try the beginning; that usually works for me," I said with a dose of faux optimism. Then, as if a joke weren't inappropriate enough, I followed it with an embarrassingly loud, insane-sounding chortle.

I resisted the urge to kick myself. I felt my face burning but, for some reason, my awkwardness seemed to give Casey the strength he needed to begin his story.

"Six years ago," he began, "well, seven now, my mom had Rosie. I was sixteen at the time and, believe me, I had no interest in sharing my house with a screaming, crying baby. But my mom didn't care. She had been trying to have another kid since I was four years old. She told me that the doctors said that she was infertile, but she knew better."

He shook his head and gave a sad little nostalgic smile that made me wish I didn't know how his story would end.

"She always used to tell me, 'Just you wait, Casey. I'm gonna give you a little brother or sister if it's the last thing I do!' And, after eleven years of trying and a horrible, difficult pregnancy that almost killed her twice, she had Rosie." He chuckled. "And you know what I did as soon as I saw that baby?"

"What?" I asked, smiling slightly.

"I cried. Sixteen years old, six-foot-two and I cried like a little girl. She was the most beautiful thing I'd ever seen, with her tiny fingers and tiny toes, and her big, beautiful blue eyes…"

Casey trailed off, his expression clouding as he skipped prematurely to the end of the tale in his mind.

"Did she have any hair?" I asked, trying to keep him focused. "A lot of babies are bald when they're born."

Casey's expression cleared as he met my gaze and realized what I was doing. "Yeah," he said with a slow grin, "she had the biggest black afro I'd ever seen."

I laughed, and Casey went back to his story.

"Anyway, like I said, I was hooked from the start. Rosie had me wrapped around her little finger before she could even walk. She used to have me read her a story every night before bed," he laughed at the memory, "she liked it because I did funny voices for each of the characters."

I wanted to cry.

"She used to sit right there on my knee when we ate dinner too," he grinned, "she didn't even have her own chair at the table!" He laughed one more time, staring down at his lap as if he could still see her there. Slowly, the smile faded from his lips and I knew that the story was about to take its tragic turn.

"I loved Rosie more than anything in the world, and so did Mom. But Dad had always been weird around her, like he didn't want to get too attached or something." He frowned. "I think maybe that's one of the reasons I spoiled her so much. I had grown up with a great dad, but hers was distant and mean. You'd never believe that they were the same person.

"Anyway, one day about six months ago, this guy showed up on the doorstep asking for Mom. I answered the door, and I said she wasn't home. I asked him who he was so I could tell her he was looking for her, but before he could answer, Rosie came over..."

Casey slowed down, his face darkening for a moment, but he fought back the anger and continued, "She was just trying to show me the new dress she'd put on her Barbie doll, but suddenly the guy freaks out.

"'That's her!' he yells, 'That's my baby!'

"I said, 'I don't think so,' and then I picked her up before he tried to grab her, but he just wasn't buying it. 'I swear on my life that that's my child!' he says, and I said 'Bullshit,' and tried to close the door in his face. But he stuck his foot between the door and the jamb and he says 'Look! Look at her eyes, man! She's got my eyes!'

"I told him to..." Casey paused, glancing sideways at me. "Well, let's just say that I told him in no uncertain terms to get lost. But he wouldn't, not until I looked at Rosie's eyes. Finally, I did what he said, which was hard to do, since Rosie was crying at that point, and I looked at her eyes and I looked at his eyes, and I'll be damned if they weren't a perfect match. Their noses too."

"Wait..." I said slowly, confused, "So your dad—"

"Wasn't her dad," Casey confirmed, his face ashen. "We found out the whole story when my mom came home and sent the guy away. She sat me and my dad down at the table and told us that, for eleven years, *she* hadn't been the one who was infertile. It had always been Dad. But she'd been afraid to tell him. She said it would 'damage his pride.'"

I had no idea where his story was going. It was all too complicated, all too dramatic to have been real.

"The guy at the door was some guy Mom had worked with before she got married, and she slept with him once afterward. Once—one single time—just to get pregnant. She was ashamed, but she had to do it, she said, because she *needed* to have another baby, just one more, as if I wasn't enough for her.

"Don't get me wrong," he added quickly, seeing my mouth open to either reassure him or chastise him, I wasn't sure which, "I'm glad she did it because it gave us Rosie. But on the other hand, if she hadn't have done that, none of this would have ever happened."

"What did your dad do when he found out?"

"What did he do after he found out that the woman he'd loved for twenty-five years had cheated on him and had a kid with another guy because he himself was impotent?" Casey asked, a crazy gleam in his dark eyes. "He did what most guys would have done, as barbaric as it may sound. He went out and beat the living shit out of that other guy. He put him in the hospital for three months."

"Geez…" I exhaled softly.

"Oh, he was just getting started. When he came home, he beat the shit out of my mom too, and he would have killed her if I hadn't tackled him first." Casey stood up then, his fingers curling into fists as he paced the bathroom. He seemed to get bigger as he got angrier, making the room feel even smaller and more claustrophobic than it already was. "He was strong," he continued, "but I was stronger. We fought for what seemed like an hour before he finally gave up and left the house."

I could feel the tension in the air as Casey got closer and closer to the inevitable end of his story. My palms were sweaty and I could feel the grasping hands of panic clutching at my own throat as I tried not to imagine what was coming next. Like a train on a track, though, there was only one way this could go, only one way it could end.

"The first thing I did was check on my mom." He stopped pacing, his face suddenly livid as he banged his enormous fist on my sink. "Dammit!" he bellowed, wiping his eyes, violently pulling at the corners of them as if he could beat the tears away. "Why didn't I check on Rosie first? She was six freaking years old!"

I stood up, agonized by his agony. I took a few tentative steps forward to take his hand, and he looked at me, his eyes so full of pain that I felt my own burn with sympathetic tears. "Why didn't I check on her first?" he whispered, asking me the question he had been torturing himself with for six long months.

He closed his haunted eyes, sending a stream of big, bulbous tears rolling down his cheeks, but I didn't have the answer he sought.

"What happened next?" I asked quietly, holding his hand as I tried to transfer whatever strength I had left to him. He had to finish his story now, he had to face his darkness, just as I would have to face mine. At first I hadn't wanted him to do it; I hadn't wanted to hear him tell his story or watch him grapple with his inner demons. But now I needed him to. If he could find the strength to overcome his past, maybe I could do it too.

"After I checked on my mom, I went to Rosie's room," he told me, his hollow, brittle voice breaking, "but she wasn't there. Her window was open, but she wasn't there. I ran to the front door, and there she was, in the car with Dad." He gave a strangled sob. "She had her nose pressed against the passenger's side window, grinning at me. And waving. She was always trying to get Dad to take her places, but he never would. I guess he had always suspected that she wasn't really his daughter."

He sniffed and wiped his face on the back of his free hand and I made to let go of the other one, but he just gripped it tighter, as if my tiny, useless hand could help him, as if it was comforting to him somehow.

"She was just sitting there in the passenger's seat, smiling and waving," he choked, "like they were going to the park or something. God, she loved the park. But then..."

I squeezed his hand and he stared down at me, and I watched his face crumple with misery as he said, "Clara, he stabbed her. In the throat. With my mom's kitchen knife."

I covered my mouth with my cast in horror as the tears finally began to stream down my own cheeks.

"There was blood...everywhere...all over the window and the seats... For a split second, she just sat there, still laughing, but just like that, the light left her eyes and she fell backward, just as my dad slit his own throat.

"I couldn't feel my legs, but somehow I made it out to the car. When I got there, the doors were locked. I broke the glass in the window and got this cut here," he said, pointing to a large, jagged, raised scar near the inside of his right elbow, the complete opposite of all the other thin, straight ones he had inflicted himself on his left. "But I was too late. Rosie was dead. She was just lying there in that pool of blood..." He gave a dry heave. "God, there was so much blood!" He gasped for air, choking on memories. "And it was my fault. I shouldn't have let him get to her. I should have known that was what he wanted. I should have—"

"It wasn't your fault," I soothed, putting my fingers to his lips to quiet him. "You couldn't have known that, no one could have."

"But I should have," he said darkly, looking over my head and into the past he could never change.

"Is that why you cut yourself?" I asked, realization dawning on me as I took my hand from his face to brush it over the scars on his left forearm, "To punish yourself?"

Casey glanced at me, then dropped his gaze to the floor, ashamed.

"You lost your dad, your family, and your baby sister," I said as I stepped closer to him, ducking to get beneath his gaze so that he would have to meet my eyes. "Don't you think you've been punished enough already?"

For a long moment, we just stared at each other, me trying to read his expression and him trying to disentangle himself from the past.

"Yeah," he said slowly, as if I had just led him to a solution that he had never considered before, "Yeah, I have."

With that, he began to cry in earnest, his shoulders shaking with earthquake-like sobs and tears raining down his crumpled face as I hugged him, wrapping my arms around his stomach as he cried into my neck, just as I had done into his at the park just a few days before. Whatever strength I had left, I willed to him, and whatever doubts I had about us needing each other faded away.

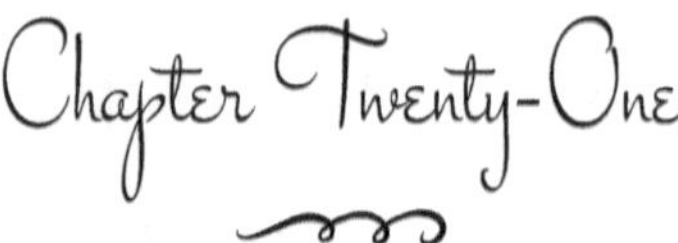

Chapter Twenty-One

"LET'S SEE, I have Cheez-its, Ravioli, a box of Kraft Macaroni and Cheese...oh, and I still have some of that ice cream from the other day..."

It was twenty minutes after Casey's bathroom confessional and we were in the kitchen. Casey was slumped, pale and defeated, at the table, and I was trying to fill the emptiness the only way I knew how anymore: with food.

"I also have a frozen pizza in the freezer, but I think that's been in there since I moved in so—"

"I've gotta get out of here," Casey declared abruptly, shoving his chair backward and getting to his feet.

"Oh...okay," I replied, blind-sided. I had been sure that the eventual sharing of our respective secrets would bring us closer together, but now, all of a sudden, he couldn't wait to get away from me.

I turned back to the cabinet so he wouldn't see the crushed expression I knew I must be wearing. I heard him stomp out of the kitchen, his combat boots plodding heavily across the linoleum and onto the living room carpet. I heard him open the front door, and my heart fell like a stone from my chest to my empty stomach.

"You coming?" he called.

It took me a moment to realize that he was talking to me, and a moment longer to realize what he was asking.

"Oh! Um...yeah," I answered, trying to keep the oddly elated feeling in my stomach from reaching my face. I grabbed my jacket from the coat rack by the door and followed him out to the parking lot, where we wordlessly mounted his motorcycle.

"WHERE ARE WE GOING?" I yelled as he started the engine, the thrilling rumbling making my inappropriate elation even worse.

"DON'T KNOW YET," he yelled back, kicking up the bulky metal kickstand.

Without another word, the bike rolled forward and we were off, traveling into the unknown at much too high a speed and much too close a proximity to each other.

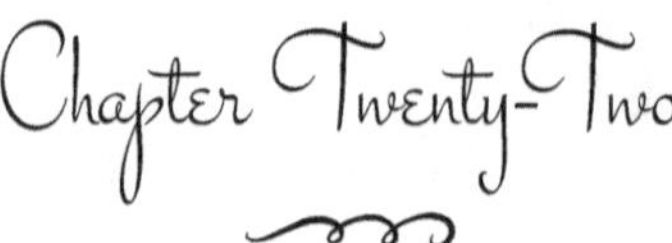

How long we were on the motorcycle, I have no idea. Somehow, despite the recurrent throbbing in my hand, the deafening roar of the earsplitting engine, and the rough, scratchy-rumbling of the thick wheels as they rolled over piles of gravel and craggy asphalt, I was lulled into a heavy doze in which I dreamt that I was riding off into the sunset behind Casey astride a large, loud, black horse. Just as dream-Casey (beautifully alive and handsome this time) turned toward me to speak, I felt a light pat on my left hand.

Blearily, I awoke and opened my eyes to find that we had stopped—something I should have noticed much sooner, for the eardrum-shattering engine noise had been replaced by the loudest silence I had ever heard in my life. Not a single cricket chirped and not a single living being breathed as the silence pressed into my ears like a pair of fuzzy earmuffs. As I took in the almost-absolute darkness around me, I instinctively clutched Casey tighter as a thrill of fear tickled my spine.

"It's okay," Casey said, patting my hand again. I could feel his deep voice rumbling through his chest just the way I had felt the bike rumble beneath me.

"Where are we?" I asked, as Casey gently extracted himself from my grip and dismounted.

"Graveyard," he replied, his voice hushed.

"Oh," I said, my sarcastic voice a bit higher than I intended it to be, "that *is* okay then."

"Come on," Casey said, a smile in his voice as he took my hand to help me off the bike, "there's something I want to show you."

I, of course, needed no more convincing.

Together, we traversed the grassy knolls of the sprawling cemetery as the first dim, orange-ish glow of dawn began to color the starless sky. Every snap of a twig or crunch of dirt beneath our feet sounded like an explosion in the muffled, muted atmosphere. Nothing moved, nothing breathed, nothing lived around us, and the silence was so profound that it felt as if we had been transported to another planet, one on which no other life form had survived. Despite the sense of lifelessness around us, I still felt the need to whisper instead of talk; it was so quiet, the only thing you could hear were your own thoughts, and even those were too loud.

I could just see my breath in a thin cloud before me as we neared a large, cordoned-off area of the graveyard full of small, granite and plaster statues of cherubs surrounded by a knee-high white picket fence.

"This is where they keep the kids," Casey told me, his voice hushed and somber.

A strange feeling, somewhere between sorrow and fear, prickled the back of my neck. There must have been fifty graves in just that section of the cemetery. Fifty lives lost before they had really even begun. Fifty bodies, each lying beneath the cold, dirty ground where they would rot and decompose and fade from the memories of everyone who had ever loved them. Just like Rosie would. Just like Charlotte would.

Just like I would.

I reached for Casey's hand in the semi-darkness, and felt his rough fingers entwine with mine as he stopped in front of a simple stone grave marker beside a short, concrete cherub playing a harp.

"We didn't have enough money to buy her an angel," Casey said softly, staring down at the tombstone. I felt a lump in my throat as I read the inscription etched into the pale grey stone.

"Rosie Estella Linderman
    October 19, 2004—March 5, 2010

Little child
    Angels Blessed
    Up in Heaven
    You now rest."

"It's beautiful," I whispered, and Casey squeezed my hand in appreciation. "I wish I had some flowers or something for her."

"Me too," Casey sighed.

For a moment, we both just stood there, hand in hand, as we both wished that things had been different for Rosie, for Charlotte, for us.

"I come here a lot," Casey said after a while, kneeling down to wipe some grass clippings off the headstone. "I know she's not here, not *really*," he continued, as if he had to explain himself to me, "but sometimes being here makes me feel less..."

"Alone," I finished, in complete understanding. I had never been able to bring myself to visit Charlotte's grave after her funeral, but I could definitely relate to the sentiment.

Casey looked up at me then, a strange expression on his shadowed face as his brown eyes glinted in the pale morning light. "Have you ever seen a sunrise?" he asked suddenly.

"I painted a sun*set* once," I told him as he sat down to the right of the tombstone and patted a patch of ground to his left, "but I've never been up early enough to see a sun*rise*," I finished, sitting down next to him.

"Good," he replied, lying back in the grass, his right arm beneath his shaggy head like a pillow and his left outstretched, inviting me to lie back as well. Suddenly shy, I awkwardly lay down beside him, my head on his bicep and my heart fluttering like a trapped bird, beating so loudly I was sure he could hear it. I shivered a bit in the chilly, too-still air, too much like that inside of a cave or a tomb, and he pulled me closer to his side. Our bodies were barely touching but instantly I was on fire, my cheeks burning and my hands sweating.

"Look there," he whispered, taking the hand out from beneath his head to point at the horizon, seemingly oblivious to my impending spontaneous combustion.

For a moment, I saw nothing but a light, goldish-orange glow. Then, it happened.

My breath caught as an enormous glowing orb of flame slowly ascended from seemingly nowhere, spreading tendrils of hot pinks and dark oranges across the pale morning sky. The few fluffy clouds that hovered above our heads were bathed in fuchsia and the dew-covered trees in the cemetery began to sparkle and glitter as if they had been sprinkled with some sort of fairy dust. In the distance, I could hear birds singing their wake-up songs and beside me I heard Casey sigh.

"What do you think?"

"It's beautiful," I whispered in awe, my voice constricted with emotion. My sunset painting had been great, but it was nothing compared to nature's own, personal masterpiece. As I lay there, wondering how I could ever possibly transfer such a spectacular scene onto canvas, Casey wrapped his arm more snugly around my shoulder and I reached up to hold his fingers as they draped over my arm.

"I've never told anyone about Rosie before," he said, still

watching the sun rise higher and higher as the sky continued to burst with even more vibrant shades of pinks, oranges and reds, "and I've never brought anyone here."

I was touched.

"I'm glad you did," I replied, referring to both events.

"Me too," Casey murmured back, kissing the top of my head again.

Lying there in the damp, dewy grass, I couldn't believe that it had been a matter of days since I had met Casey. I couldn't believe that I had missed out on having someone like him in my life for so long because of my own fear of either hurting or getting hurt. Most of all, though, I couldn't believe that I had gone my whole life without ever really seeing a sunrise.

Chapter Twenty-Three

IF THERE WAS one thing I had learned about grief, it was that it took a lot out of you. Whether it's the stress of not knowing whether or not you are going to burst into tears the next moment or just the general strain of carrying the weight of the world around on your aching shoulders twenty-four/seven, it is tiring. That is why, at nine thirty that same morning, Casey and I were found, fast asleep, on the grass in the middle of the children's section of the cemetery by a large, angry funeral procession.

"Ahem!"

I jerked awake, bashing myself in the nose with my cast. Squinting through watery eyes, I saw the red, puffy-eyed faces of about two dozen black-garbed mourners staring down at us with mingled looks of surprise and disgust.

"Uh, Casey?" I said slowly, keeping my eye on the angriest member of the procession, an elderly priest with a large crucifix in one hand and a thick black Bible in the other—either of which would have been perfect for bashing our sleepy heads in. His wrinkled face was contorted with a fury I'd never seen on a man of God before. If I had to guess, I would have said that it was the same look he reserved for the devil himself.

Casey muttered something unintelligible and wrapped his arms more tightly around me. I squirmed, smiling apologetically at the glowering priest as I tried to wake him up.

Judging by the scandalized look on many of their faces, the mourners obviously thought that Casey and I had been doing something much more sinful than lying in the grass watching the sun rise, and we were in no position to defend ourselves. Although we had, in truth, done nothing more than sleep, we were now so tangled up in each other that even I wondered whether or not we had crossed some sort of line. Both of Casey's massive arms were wrapped around me, holding me close to his chest. My good arm was threaded beneath his right armpit and my hand was in his hair —something I quickly remedied before the priest's already narrowed eyes could narrow any further. Our legs were in a complicated knot—his left leg under mine, my right over his—and my face was so close to his chest that I could smell his sweat and hear the slow, steady thud of his heart.

"Th—this isn't what it looks like," I sputtered, poking Casey in the arm. Man he was a sound sleeper. "We weren't—you know —*doing* anything, we were just—"

"What time is it?" Casey yawned, his eyes still closed, oblivious to our predicament as he nestled his face further into my messy hair.

"Nine thirty-four," drawled the priest, his arms crossed.

Casey bolted upright, bowling me over in the process.

"Sorry," he winced, reaching over to help me. Already embarrassed by our intimacy in the presence of a group of mourning strangers, I waved his hand away and sat up of my own accord, my face burning. "Sorry, Father," Casey added, getting to his feet.

I stood up as well, trying to think of something to say to the priest that would make him stop glaring daggers at me. In the end, I went with something that sounded a little like "God bless your loss" and Casey and I scampered off, our heads bowed in shame as we hurried away from the funeral and back to Casey's dew-slick motorcycle, where Casey did something I didn't expect.

He laughed.

It began as a quiet, introspective chuckle as he replayed the scene in his mind, but soon his laughter grew into large, booming guffaws that were as contagious as they were loud. All of the sadness of the night before was replaced by a joyous cacophony I had never imagined could come from a man who had endured so much pain. I had heard him laugh before, but not like that. His previous laughs had always been tinged with a touch of melancholy or guilt, as if he, like me, was afraid that laughter might be considered inappropriate for a person in our current stage of grief. But this time his laughter was cheerful and loose; it was happy, it was free, and I couldn't help but join in.

We laughed for a good ten minutes, interjecting breathless impressions of the priest's angry face and formal, lilting voice until, finally, we both ran out of air and energy and collapsed onto the pavement, clutching our sore stomachs as we leaned against Casey's bike.

"Are you as hungry as I am right now?" Casey panted, wiping tears of laughter from his eyes.

"I think I'm even hungrier," I replied. Just then, my stomach growled audibly, as if to support my previous statement.

"Good," Casey nodded, casually reaching over to tuck a loose strand of hair behind my ear and giving me goose bumps, "Let's go get something to eat."

Chapter Twenty-Four

"TELL ME SOMETHING," said Casey, through a mouthful of Denny's best gravy-smothered breakfast sausage.

"Like what?" I replied, trying to ram another enormous bite of syrup-soaked pancakes past my already-sticky lips.

"Anything."

"Dat wuz helbful," I said thickly, smirking.

"Something about you," Casey clarified, swallowing, "Something you like, something you hate. Something I don't already know." He held his fork like a microphone and did a passable Matt Lauer impression. "Tell me, who *is* Clara Halpert?"

I giggled, but as he held the fork mic out to me, the humor in the situation seemed to slowly dissipate.

Who is *Clara Halpert?* I wondered, as if I had never asked myself that question before. Was she the sad, mopey girl that had sat alone in her apartment every night for the last four months, reliving her tortured past? Or was she the girl who was so sick of herself that she had broken her own hand just to feel something? Maybe she was the girl who threw up in public, or the girl who had nearly been raped in the park because of her own crappy judgment. Or maybe she was just a horrible sister and a—

No, I thought, feeling the panic start to rise in my chest as Casey waited patiently for an answer I didn't have. I didn't want to be any of those things, I couldn't be!

But I was. I was all of them. I could remember no Clara Halpert from before the incident at the lake. It was like an attack of amnesia, severing me not only from the painful parts of my past, but from the joyous parts as well. Surely I had once been different. Surely I had once been better!

Who was Clara Halpert? Where had she gone? Did she even still exist?

There was no air in the room. The once-pleasant syrup scent was suddenly strangling me and the four pancakes I had just eaten felt like four large, heavy bricks in my churning stomach.

"I—" I began, "I...I really don't—"

"Hey," Casey said, setting down his fork and grabbing my sweaty hand.

My eyes darted to the door. I had to get out of there. I had to get out of my own head.

"Clara, it's alright."

I glanced at Casey's worried face and made a "pfft" sound of dismissal. What did he know? He had had six or seven months to heal and to rediscover his old self! I'd barely had half that! Plus, he was tough and rugged and easy-going, things I could never even pretend to be. It may have been alright for him, but it wasn't for me. It couldn't be.

I tried to wrench my damp hand out of his, but he only gripped it tighter and leaned across the table, across both of our plates to put his other hand on my cheek, his thumb just below my left eye.

"Listen to me, Clara," he said. I was so startled by his gesture and his closeness that I focused on his face and unintentionally stopped hyperventilating. "I know it's scary to let someone in. Trust me, I know that better than anyone. But believe me, whoever you were, whoever you are, whoever you want to be, is okay."

My breathing was ragged as I studied his beard, his lips, his wide nose, his strangely intense stare. "But what if I don't know any of that stuff anymore?" I asked, my voice small.

It was almost painful to be so vulnerable with someone, and the few milliseconds it took him to think of a reply seemed like a lifetime.

"Then I'll help you figure it out," he said finally, with a crooked smile that nearly stopped my already-overworked heart. "Okay?"

"Okay," I repeated weakly, and he stroked my cheek before returning his big hand, somewhat reluctantly it seemed, to his side of the table.

"Good," he said, grabbing a clean napkin and taking out the Sharpie he had apparently stolen from McDonald's two days ago. "We can start by making a list."

I watched, biting my syrupy lip as he made two vertical columns on the napkin, dividing them with a thick, lopsided line down the middle. Above one column, in the same handwriting that now covered my cast, Casey wrote "Things Clara Likes." Above the other, he wrote, "Things Clara Doesn't Like."

"Okay," he said, looking up at me, "Well, from what I have seen of you so far, I know that you like to eat."

"I love to eat," I amended quietly, a bit embarrassed. I had never been analyzed before, though I couldn't say that the sensation was entirely unpleasant.

Casey grinned. "Alright, I'll put it in the 'likes' column."

I read the list upside down as he wrote "FOOD" in all caps, and added in smaller letters beneath it, "esp. ravioli and pancakes."

He put the marker to his chin and looked at me again, squinting thoughtfully. "Hmmm...what else?"

I shrugged, but gave him an encouraging smile.

"Oh, I see." He grinned again, "You're going to make me do all the work!"

I nodded bashfully, and he gave a heavy sigh of faux-resignation.

"Alright, Clara Halpert...likes food, check. Oh! I've got it. 'Dislikes therapists and their preppy shoes'..."

I snorted so loud that an elderly woman at the table nearest to us jumped and looked up at us, appalled.

"'Likes making old ladies mad'..." Casey mumbled under his breath, smiling broadly now, "'Dislikes walls so much that she punches them'..."

By that point, I was laughing so hard that my eyes were watering and my face was burning. Somehow, Casey was once again taking what I had previously viewed as fatal flaws and was turning them into nothing more than comedic misadventures.

"'Likes laughing at Casey Linderman's lame jokes,'" Casey continued, "I like that one. And bright orange casts, you like those too..."

"And painting," I added, getting caught up in the moment and nearly forgetting what a fragile relationship I had with my craft at the moment.

"I like that one too," Casey told me, his smile becoming less humorous and more genuine somehow. For a moment, he just looked at me, an odd light in his coffee-colored eyes.

Before he could speak again, the waitress brought us our check, and we both looked down at it, blushing.

After a quick squabble over who would pay the bill, Casey snatched the receipt from me and threw down his money before I could even get my wallet out of my back pocket, which was lucky, since I still didn't have any money on me.

As we stood up to leave, one of Charlotte's old dating tips swam out of the murky depths of my memory. "If he pays," she had told me, a girlish twinkle in her eye, "it's definitely a date."

This thought made my stomach a bit queasy, so I put it out of my mind for the moment as I followed Casey out the door.

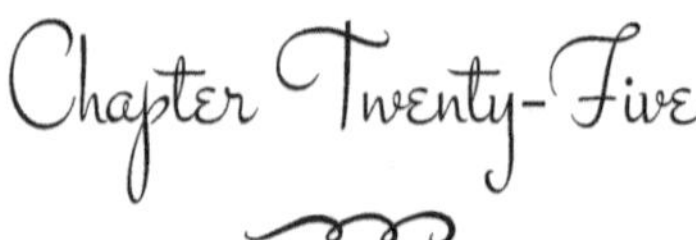

Chapter Twenty-Five

It was decidedly warmer outside when we exited the restaurant, but I still regretted not bringing a thicker jacket. My right arm was safe in its protective plaster shell, but goose bumps sprang up along my left as the unseasonably-crisp autumn air bit right through my pink-striped sweatshirt.

"So," I asked Casey as we meandered across the macadam towards his motorcycle, "What's on your agenda for today?"

"Not much," he replied, fishing in his pockets for his keys. My mind briefly jumped to the missing blanket scrap that was currently stashed in my bedroom but, once again, he didn't seem to notice its absence. "I just thought I'd hang out with this cute girl I met at Group the other day."

I blushed as he gave me a sly look, as if to judge my reaction before he said anything else.

"Oh really?" I recovered, "Do I know her?"

Casey leaned against the black leather seat of his motorcycle, his head cocked slightly to one side, as if he were appraising me. "You wanna drive?"

"What?" I asked, thrown for a loop by the interruption of our (admittedly dorky) banter.

"Do you want to drive?" he asked again, holding his keys out to me. I noticed that another purple flower barrette hung from his key ring, matching the one he wore on his boot.

"I've never driven a motorcycle before," I stammered, shaking my head. Surely he wasn't serious.

"So?"

"*So*, I don't want to wreck it! And what about this?" I held up my cast, wiggling my swollen purple fingers at him for emphasis before adding, "You can't steer a motorcycle with one hand."

Casey shrugged. "That's not a problem, I can steer for you."

"Then what would I do? Watch out for oncoming traffic?"

"That, and control the gas," he said. "Whoever controls the gas controls the bike."

I squinted at him for a moment, trying to figure him out.

"Why do you want me to drive so badly?" I asked, suspicious.

He shrugged again. "Research," he said simply, "for the list. We already know that you like *riding* motorcycles, but you can't know if you like them as a whole unless you've driven one yourself."

I thought about it for a moment, trying to find a hole in his argument. In all honesty, I was more terrified of being in control of his bike than I had ever been of riding it. Things that I was in charge of didn't normally turn out too well, and I didn't want to ruin something else that wasn't mine to ruin in the first place.

"Wait, how do you know I like riding your motorcycle?" I stalled, seeing a possible loophole. "I never said that. Maybe I just ride it because I have no other means of transportation available to me at the moment!"

"You like it," Casey assured me, with a hint of smugness in his crooked smile.

"What gave you that idea?" I countered, trying to keep him from seeing right through me, but secretly enjoying watching him try.

"Well, for one thing, if you didn't like it, you wouldn't keep riding it," he reasoned.

"Just because I ride it doesn't mean I like it," I persisted.

"Clara, you fell asleep on it this morning." Casey grinned, knowing full well that he had me. "If you weren't comfortable on a bike, there's no way that ever would have happened."

In reality, it was Casey that I was comfortable with, not the motorcycle, but I didn't have the nerve to tell him that. So I tried and failed to think of a sassy comeback, then I just gave in and admitted defeat.

"Alright, you win," I sighed. "Give me the keys."

Chapter Twenty-Six

AFTER A LONG, boring explanation of the specifications and usages of every single piece of the Kawasaki from Casey and an even longer explanation of my perceived incompetence from me, Casey finally convinced me to get on the motorcycle.

"Put your foot here," he instructed, pushing my dirty right sneaker onto one of the bike's shiny silver pedals with his mammoth black boot. "Good. Now put the other one here..."

I did as he instructed. I put a shaky hand on the left side of the handle bar, trying to convince myself that I was sitting on my safe, sturdy old ten-speed instead of a rumbling, roaring death machine. Casey put his right hand on the handlebar and gearshift mechanism and lifted a leg to swing his body over the bike to sit heavily down behind me, spawning a cacophony of worrisome creaking from the bike's springs and joints. In spite of the low temperature, I instantly felt warmer as he leaned against my back, seemingly closer than necessary.

"Okay," he said, his breath blowing my hair and tickling my ear as he leaned over my left shoulder, his scruffy face so close I could feel his beard stubble on my cheek, "Now put your cast hand on top of mine and I'll put my other hand on the other handlebar too, just in case."

"Just in case of what?" I asked, finding it a little hard to breathe.

"In case you need help," he replied, putting his large, warm, rough hand over mine. There were still scratches and bloody scabs on his knuckles from his fight with my mugger, and there was black grease under and around most of his fingernails but, for a moment, all I could do was stare at his rough, calloused hand and think about how perfect it looked next to my small, fragile, permanently paint-speckled one. My mind grew a bit fuzzy as once again I was reminded of what we could be if we could both manage to be sane individuals at the same time.

Casey must have been suffering from a similar brain fog, for the silence between us grew thick and hazy with meaning and expectation as he slowly wove his strong, tanned fingers between my pale white ones, creating a beautiful tapestry that made me want to get off the motorcycle and go paint.

I had never driven a motorcycle before, so I wasn't completely sure, but I was fairly certain that hand-holding of that nature was not normally involved.

Casey must have realized this as well, for suddenly he cleared his throat and said, much too loudly and much too gruffly, "Okay! Then if you just put your other hand there and—"

"Casey Linderman," said a voice from our left. It was a statement, not a question—an accusation, not a greeting—and it startled us both.

Casey snatched his hand away from mine as if we had just been caught doing something indecent, and I turned to see one of the last people in the world that either of us wanted to run into. As he walked toward us from the Denny's entrance, the man threw us a smug, snarky smile, as if he knew that he was ruining our moment and any hopes we had had for a pleasant morning.

"Doctor Jay," Casey growled, with an inflection that sounded like it should have ended with "if that *is*, in fact, your real name."

I felt my breath start to quicken. I had never been a fan of confrontation, but since the day Charlotte died, even the slightest hint of an oncoming argument or scuffle sent me straight into the greedy arms of panic. Casey must have felt the change in my respiration and attitude, for he took the hand that had been holding mine off the handlebar and wrapped his arm protectively around my waist.

"What do you want?" Casey demanded, not wasting any time with pleasantries.

"Nothing," Dr. Jay shrugged, an odd, knowing gleam in his droopy brown eyes, "Nothing at all. I'm just glad to see that you two are alive after the way you took off so recklessly the other night."

In spite of his snappy turquoise sweater vest and snazzy, electric-blue sneakers, the doctor seemed menacing to me. His severely parted hair and his impeccably neat clothing seemed to be covering up some sinister energy he had been penning up, and was about to release onto us.

"We're fine," Casey informed him shortly, sticking the key into the motorcycle's ignition.

"I can see that," he replied, looking down at Casey's hand on my hip. Casey didn't move it. Instead, he clutched me tighter, as if in rebellion. "You two have been together this whole time haven't you? Ever since you left the YMCA?"

"So what if we have?" Casey growled.

Doctor Jay grinned like a Cheshire cat, as if he were teasing us. "You know, relationships built on traumatic experiences never last. Haven't you ever seen *Speed*?"

I wasn't sure what he was going for by taunting us, but I was growing more and more uncomfortable by the minute. I wished Casey would just turn the key and start the engine so we could run away from our problems again. Though, to be honest, that hadn't been working very well for us so far.

"We don't care what you have to say," Casey spat, suddenly surprisingly angry. His grip on my waist was almost too tight as his arm tensed up and he clenched his fist as if he were about to punch someone.

"Well that's always been obvious!" Dr. Jay exploded, leaping over to stand in front of the bike, looming over me as he grabbed the handlebars. I moved my hands, but his face was still inches from mine as I recoiled into Casey, my panic growing exponentially as my mind threatened to take me back to that day at the lake when Davidson's face had been so close to mine that I could smell his breath and feel the sweaty, excited heat of madness oozing out of his pores.

I almost closed my eyes.

"It's been obvious that I've been nothing but a joke to you two from the start! You don't care what I have to say—you don't care what anyone has to say, even if it might be helpful to you!"

The parking lot was spinning as flecks of the therapist's spittle hit me in the face. I tried to look away from his hard, angry glare, but I couldn't. It wasn't the panic that paralyzed me, however. It was the miniscule glint of earnest sincerity and hurt in his angry eyes that made me wonder if maybe we really had done something wrong after all. Lately, all I had cared about were my own feelings and maybe Casey's, but it was possible that perhaps someone else had feelings that I could hurt as well. Maybe Dr. Jay wasn't an insensitive idiot. Maybe he was just a crappy therapist who had nevertheless always had our best interests at heart. Maybe he had genuinely been trying to help us in his own intense, scary, traumatizing way.

"Did you know that I got fired that night?" he asked.

My stomach clenched in guilt. Finally, an emotion I could understand.

"It's normal for patients to leave after one session and not come back for the next, but never, in the history of the program, has an entire therapy group gotten up and walked out of the room in the middle of a session. After you two left, the rest of the group followed suit. It makes sense—why stay if you can leave anytime you want?" he asked, beginning to sound a bit hysterical. "Do you know how that made me look in front of my boss?"

He paused for a moment, as if he were really waiting for an answer. Casey fidgeted uncomfortably with the hem of my jacket and I knew that he, too, had been sufficiently cowed.

"Like a dumbass," Dr. Jay answered himself, "A dumbass who isn't even competent enough in his field to conduct a simple group therapy session."

"I'm sorry," I squeaked, my voice small as I was finally able to look away from his eyes and down at my hands in my lap.

"You should be," he replied, but this was immediately followed by a sigh of resignation as he lost all pretense of anger. "I just wanted to get through to people," he said dejectedly, taking his hands off the handlebars and taking a step back. "I could have helped you, you know," he said, and a small part of me believed him.

"Just promise me one thing before I go," he said, his authoritative voice almost pleading, "Just promise me that you two will at least share your traumatic experiences with each other, if you haven't already? I know you don't want to talk about it in front of a group of strangers or an over-enthusiastic dumbass like me, but at least share it with each other. I meant what I said at Group. The first step to overcoming your grief is to share your story with someone else. You guys have no idea how much better you'll feel just knowing that you don't have to carry that burden all by yourself."

Dr. Jay looked at Casey, who quickly said, "I promise."

Then he looked at me, his brown eyes expectant and kind this time. In spite of my reservations, my panic, and my fear, I whispered, "I promise too."

Chapter Twenty-Seven

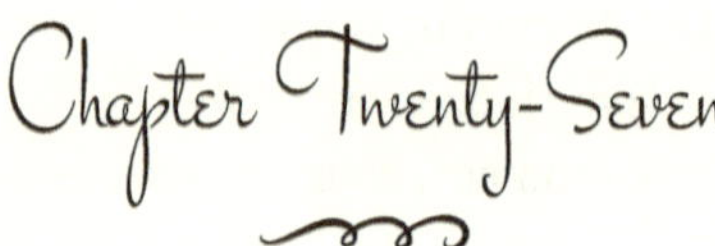

"Things Clara does not like..." Casey said, pinching the cap of his marker between his teeth as he took out his list a few minutes later, "'Therapists that interrupt our motorcycle lesson and make us feel like crap'."

We had decided to postpone the remainder of my driving lesson until Casey and I felt less like jerks. Instead, we had chosen to walk down the street to a Home Depot, where Casey wanted to pick up a few vague-sounding supplies to fix up the garage.

As we walked in, we were greeted by the cold, grey-concrete floor and drab, minimalistic, grey stone décor that working men apparently found appealing. There was hardly a soul in sight in the hardware store at ten thirty on a Thursday morning, and the only noises we heard were our own footsteps echoing against the floor and the strangely ominous sounding Bob Dylan song, "Knockin' on Heaven's Door" playing over the sound system.

"The paint's right over here," Casey said, leading the way to the largest aisle in the store. I followed mutely, mulling over the day's events as I looked down at my shoes.

"What kind of paint are you looking for?" I asked listlessly as I shuffled one of my sneakers onto the top of the other while he studied the wall of rainbow-colored paint sample cards.

On another day in another life, I would have been driven insane by the pure possibilities inherent an aisle full of such bright, beautiful colors, but at the moment, I was too depressed to look at anything other than the slick grey industrial floor beneath my feet.

I had always planned on telling Casey the whole story of what had happened to Charlotte, but suddenly it seemed like I had been given an ultimatum. The guilt I felt for ruining Dr. Jay's career only intensified the potency of the promise I had made him, the promise I wasn't so sure that I could keep, especially now that the entire of memory of that day had begun to seep back into my consciousness in a way that it never had before. The closer I got to Casey, the less I wanted him to know what exactly had happened, what exactly I had done.

"I'm not sure," Casey replied thoughtfully, seemingly oblivious to my moodiness, "What do you think about this one?"

Reluctantly, I glanced up to see him holding up a can of intensely, hideously, violently bright orange paint that almost put my cast to shame.

I laughed out loud as Bob Dylan began his solemn dirge a second time.

"What?" Casey asked, with faux incredulity, "You don't like it?"

"No, I love it," I assured him, taking the eight ounce can from him and reading the label to find out what one called such an exotic, eccentric color.

"Blazing Tangerine," apparently.

"'*Blazing Tangerine*'?" I snorted, "What part of the garage are you going to paint with this?"

"I dunno," he said, shrugging. There was a mischievous gleam in his eye not unlike the one I had first seen at our second Group session and I wondered if he was getting ready to tell me more about his brother Sally and the stampeding unicorns. "What about this one?"

I took a can of electric blue paint from him. "'Azure Supernova'," I read, grinning, "That will be a great complementary color for your 'Blazing Tangerine'."

"Good," he replied, nodding in satisfaction.

He grabbed an empty cart that someone had left behind near the painter's tape and put both cans in it.

"How do you feel about 'Screamin' Saffron'?"

"Too close to 'Blazing Tangerine'," I decided.

"'Rockin' Rosacea'?"

I approved the pinkish-purple paint with the possibly offensive name, as well as four others ('Purple Poison,' 'Crimson Crash,' 'Emerald Explosion,' and plain old 'Blue Velvet') before I felt compelled to ask again, "What are you planning to paint with all this stuff?"

"Nothing," Casey said simply, moving over to the paintbrushes.

"Then why are you buying it?" I asked, completely baffled as I trailed behind him like a lost puppy, waiting to see if he'd throw me a bone and let me in on his plan.

"Well, I have this artist friend, see," he said, fanning the bristles on a narrow-handled flat brush, "and I was thinking of hiring her to paint me a mural on the inside wall of my garage. I don't think she'll go for it though," he said, putting down that brush and picking up a bigger one, "I don't think she likes me too much."

I froze.

Did he realize what he was asking me? Did he realize that it had been months since I had painted—truly, honestly, earnestly painted—anything other than a few little pink bunnies on a blanket that I'd probably never even show him? He was asking me to break the most extensive creative block I'd ever had, as if it were as simple as picking out paints with funny names and paintbrushes with the softest bristles and smiling at me with that sweet, crooked smile.

He wasn't just asking me to paint, he was asking me to become responsible for something, to become someone that someone else depended on. The last time someone had depended on me, I had let them down in every possible way. I wasn't sure that I could risk that happening again, especially since that time I would not only be letting Casey down, I'd be letting myself down as well.

"I'll take that silence as a 'no'," he said with a nervous chuckle as he put the brush back on the shelf.

"What if it's not any good?" I asked, my voice so quiet that I wasn't sure that he had heard me, but I was too scared and self-conscious to repeat it.

Bob Dylan sang his second chorus for the seventh time as I looked down at Casey's boots. At one time, I had been sure that my art was good, and I'd have defended it to my very last breath. But now...now it suddenly seemed that nothing I ever did was good enough, or would ever be good enough again. Not only had Davidson shattered my life, he had shattered my self-confidence as well.

"Then I'll help you paint over it and start again," Casey said softly, leaving the cart behind and walking over to me. "I don't really care what it looks like, to be honest. All I care about is you getting to paint again. By the look on your face when you talk about painting, I can tell that you love it and you miss it. Artists are artists for life, and they should always have a chance to pursue that. It doesn't matter if the mural is good or bad or weird or scary; anything you paint will be good enough for me."

I looked up into his sincere, soulful brown eyes and I felt another small piece of the wall of guilt and pain and sadness that had enclosed my battered heart chip off and fall away as Charlotte's words traveled through time and filtered though Casey. Although I hadn't known it until then, they were exactly the words I had been needing to hear.

Before I could stop myself, I leapt up and hugged him, throwing my arms around his neck without caring if any of the invisible store clerks saw. Fortunately, after a split second of shock, Casey reciprocated the gesture with interest, squeezing me tight and lifting me up off my feet for a moment before depositing me back where I'd started, my face ten shades redder and my heavy heart ten pounds lighter.

"I knew I'd get you with that 'Azure Supernova,'" he said with a grin, winking at me as he brushed my bangs out of my eyes again.

"It was actually the 'Rockin' Rosacea,'" I joked weakly, grinning back as the butterflies in my stomach fluttered painfully beneath the layers of pancakes I had eaten earlier.

Casey stared down at me for a moment, and Bob Dylan began his ballad once again.

"I think their Muzak is broken," I said awkwardly, feeling self-conscious as my face continued to burn.

Casey remained silent for a moment, studying me again as I glanced around at the suddenly beautiful rainbow-colored paint cards on the wall. Then he said something that I never saw coming.

"You wanna dance?"

"What?" I asked, flabbergasted.

"This song is starting to grow on me," he said, shrugging in such an adorable way that I was pretty sure my already-pounding heart would explode, "and I'd really like to dance with you."

"Oh," I said stupidly. I hesitated for a moment, glancing around at the two or three sales associates that had chosen that moment to finally appear and wander up and down the aisles, as if keeping an eye on us.

"Here?" I asked doubtfully, though I had to admit that the thought of a slow dance with Casey was growing more and more appealing by the second.

"Yep," he said, taking my hand as Bob Dylan begged his momma to put his guns in the ground again, since he couldn't shoot them anymore anyway. "Right here."

Before I could accept or reject his invitation, he pulled me in close, one arm around my waist and one hand holding my cast to his heart. My chest pressed against his as the music swelled, and I laid my head on his bicep as the too-short song ended and began anew.

Slowly, we pivoted in a small circle and Casey put his scruffy cheek against mine. Softly, sweetly, his deep timbre sending shivers up and down my spine, Casey began to sing along, his lips brushing my ear and sending thousands of tiny tingles throughout my entire body.

As the paint cards and the brushes and the bascarts all disappeared around us, I prayed that song would go on forever.

Chapter Twenty-Eight

AN HOUR LATER, we were back at my apartment. Casey was heating up a family-sized can of Beefaroni on the stove and I had gone down the hall to the bedroom to change out of my rumpled, slept-in, graveyard-dirt-covered clothes. After a few more turns around the paint can aisle, a Home Depot employee had finally fixed the sound system, and neither of us had felt much like dancing to the B52's "Love Shack." Although Bob Dylan's song had ended long ago, it was still playing in my head as I pulled off my t-shirt and replaced it with a clean, bright, yellow and white-striped sweater with three-quarter-length sleeves.

As I was shimmying into another pair of faded, fraying blue jeans, something on the floor brushed against my sock feet and I looked down to see the blanket I had made for Casey, covered in tempera-paint bunnies and wadded up in anger.

I picked it up, turning it over and around in my hands as I tried to decide whether to show it to Casey or not. It was not my best work, not by a long shot, but I had spent a lot of time on it. It had helped me to chip away at the wall that my creativity was hiding behind, and part of me wanted Casey to enjoy it as much as I had. However, by giving the blanket to Casey, I would be admitting that I had stolen—not just taken, stolen—his most valued possession.

"Lunch is ready, milady," Casey called from the kitchen in a horrible impersonation of a British accent (or was it French?).

I hesitated.

On one hand, he might think the blanket was cool and would be happy to have it. On the other hand, he might be pissed that he'd probably spent the past few days looking everywhere for Rosie's blanket swatch, only to find out that I'd had it all along.

"Clara?"

"Coming!" I said shrilly, folding the blanket up neatly and holding it behind my back as I opened the bedroom door and stepped into the hallway.

When I got to the kitchen, Casey was ladling heaping, mountain-sized portions of pasta into the two plastic bowls he must have washed while he was waiting for lunch to boil.

He looked up and smiled when I came in, and I noticed that he had somehow gotten a long, thick smear of red sauce across his left cheek. He looked like a proud little boy who had just cooked his own dinner for the first time. I couldn't help but return his grin as the butterflies in my stomach kicked into overdrive.

"Dinner is served," Casey said with a bow, a paper towel draped over his folded arm as he skirted around me to pull out my chair.

"It smells delicious," I said truthfully as I took a step toward the table and tried not to drool.

"Whatcha got there?" he asked, wiping his hands on the towel as he pointed at mine.

The moment of truth had come, but suddenly I wasn't ready.

"Oh, um..."

There were a thousand reasons why I shouldn't show him the blanket, and they were all clamoring to be the first to come out of my dry, cottony mouth.

"It's uh..."

Casey looked puzzled as I began to stammer incoherently. His dark brows were knitted slightly and his chocolate-colored eyes were still smiling kindly down at me as he waited for an explanation for my odd behavior. Right then, I realized that it was useless to try to hide things from Casey, no matter what my own insecurities were. He would get the truth out of me sooner or later, just like he had at the diner. I had spent the past four months—as well as much of the past twenty years—trying to pull away from people, and he was the only one who had ever tried to stop me. He was the only one who had held on when everyone else had found it easier to just let go. He deserved the blanket, just like he deserved the truth.

"Here," I said simply, thrusting the blanket at him before I could change my mind.

As he took it from me, I tried to wring my hands in agitation, but only managed to scratch my palm on my cast.

Looking a bit surprised, he unfolded it and took in, one by one, the frolicking bunnies. I watched his eyes move from my paintings to the scrap from the original blanket and I panicked.

"I'm sorry!" I burst, "That piece of Rosie's blanket fell out of your pocket at McDonald's the other day and I picked it up, thinking I could fix it, but I couldn't! I tried! I scrubbed and I scrubbed and I scrubbed, but the blood just wouldn't come out!"

My voice was getting higher and higher and faster and faster as I tried to explain while he just stared at me, completely silent, with a strange look in his eye that I hoped was not bordering on hatred.

"So I thought, 'why not make Casey a new blanket?' So I found the paint and the fabric and I was up all night making it— not that it was hard, it's just that I can't paint as well with my left hand, see? Plus, I hadn't painted for months...but anyway, I know it doesn't replace Rosie's real blanket, but I thought maybe it—"

My blabbering was abruptly cut off as Casey dropped the blanket and kissed me, his hands on my face and in my hair as he pulled me in close. At first I was startled, but I quickly gave in and closed my eyes as I was swept away by the scent of Beefaroni and motorcycle exhaust and the feel of his soft lips against mine.

Just as I was really starting to enjoy myself, however, Casey pulled back, his hands still on my cheeks, his big thumbs stroking my curls.

"Sorry," he said, a bit breathlessly, his already-ruddy face flushed, "I've just been wanting to do that all day."

"So...you're not mad at me?" I asked, once my voice started working again.

"I'm not mad."

"And you liked the blanket?"

"It's beautiful," he said softly, leaning in for another kiss, "*You're* beautiful."

"And *you* have Beefaroni on your face," I whispered, grinning, as our lips met again.

Chapter Twenty-Nine

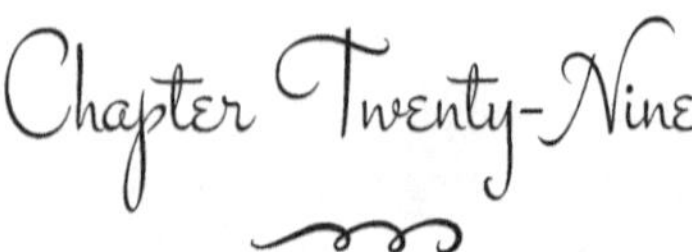

AFTER FINISHING a lunch I couldn't really taste, on a stomach that wouldn't settle, Casey talked me into showing him some of my old paintings.

"I need to see some samples of your work before I let you loose in my garage," he had teased.

It was less his words than the feel of his big, rough fingers between mine that convinced me to let him into the bedroom, where my past had gone to die four months earlier.

As he sat amongst the wadded-up clothes and blankets draped over the twin-sized mattress I never used, I pulled open the white-slatted folding doors on the closet, revealing a dozen cardboard boxes and my artwork graveyard. Rolls and rolls of scrolls and canvases filled the back corner of the tiny space, and I could feel a shift in the air as I revisited the works I had never really intended to look at again.

Just like before, the room slowly fogged with memories and all at once, I was back in the studio where my dream had been shattered, along with the only life I had ever known.

I had gone to the studio to work out some of my anger and hurt feelings after my fight with Charlotte over Davidson, and I had pulled a square of blank, white canvas out of my small locker to place on my easel.

As I lifted the canvas, however, I noticed that there was already a painting on the tripod. Frowning, I realized that it was one of Professor Davidson's macabre mannequin pieces. Like most of the others, this mannequin was dismembered, with one arm dangling from a nearby tree and another lying near the edge of what looked like some sort of lake or pond.

I put down my canvas and stepped closer, feeling vaguely afraid but not knowing why. Even more so than usual, there was something ominous in the dark, menacing blue, black, and grey hues and the straight, razor-sharp brush strokes of Davidson's painting. There was a small, black shed in the back of the frame beneath a sky full of swirling black clouds, and there was a glimmer of cold, harsh yellow light shining from one of its tiny windows. The lake was dark blue and choppy, and the perspective of the piece was such that the mannequin corpse's face could be seen clearly as she floated, face-up and glassy-eyed, in the middle of it. Her pretty white sundress and long, beautiful, blonde hair fanned out around her and I felt the icy hand of fear clutch my heart.

My eyes darted back to the mannequin's pale, porcelain face and I knew in that moment that something horrible had happened.

"Are you alright?" Casey asked, sounding worried as he sat up on the bed, causing the rusty springs to squeak and groan.

"Yeah," I gasped, shaking my head to try to clear it out. "Yeah, I'm fine."

I brought a trembling hand to my forehead and rubbed it back and forth, as if I could erase the memory of that painting from my brain with it.

"Are you sure?" Casey persisted. "Because we don't have to do this now if you don't want to."

"No, I want to," I said, more firmly and convincingly this time.

As if rebelling against my own psyche, I snatched a handful of rolled-up canvases and walked over on unsteady legs to sit Indian-style on the bed next to Casey. I put the rolls down in front of us and sat back against the cold, bare pillow, taking a deep breath.

"I haven't looked at these since before my sister Charlotte died," I told him, as if I were preparing him for a major emotional disaster.

"Can I ask why?" Casey inquired quietly, putting his arm around my waist—a gesture that never failed to make me feel safer, even if the only real danger was coming from my own subconscious.

"My art professor is the one that killed her," I said, a current of cold bitterness rippling beneath my voice.

"Jesus," Casey muttered, squeezing my waist tighter as he ran his free hand though his shaggy hair. What had started off as a playful, light-hearted enterprise had suddenly taken a dark and depressing turn, and I felt bad. I was on the verge of apologizing for my perceived overreaction when he said, "Look, we really don't have to do this right now if you're not ready. I don't want to force you into anything."

"No," I said shaking my head, "it's time. It's past time. I'm tired of letting him ruin my life."

"Okay," Casey exhaled, leaning over to kiss me on the top of the head, "then let's do it."

With uncertain, shaky fingers I removed the rubber band that held the first roll of canvas in a tightly wound tube and watched with trepidation as it began to unfurl of its own accord. I took another deep breath and clumsily flattened it out across my lap. Suddenly, as I held the stubbornly curling paper up with a trembling hand, my anxiety was replaced by a warm, tender feeling I had never expected to feel toward my artwork again.

"It's Charlotte," I whispered in awe, tears springing to my eyes. For the first time in what felt like a lifetime of crying, my tears were neither bitter nor sad. They were, instead, the happy tears of a girl who had just realized that maybe her missing sister was not as far away as she seemed.

I chuckled quietly as I ran a finger over the portrait that I had painted when I was in high school. The paint-and-paper Charlotte was hanging upside down on a swing in our backyard, her arms looped around the rusty silver chains and her yellow-blonde hair falling loose all around her as she stuck her rosy pink tongue out at me, her sky blue eyes sparkling with laughter—a pose the real Charlotte had held dutifully for an hour and a half before pretending to pass out and fall off the swing with a flurry of girlish giggling.

The girl in my painting—the free-spirited, lovable, young-hearted older sister—was the Charlotte I had been missing. For months, the only Charlotte I could recall was the one who had been bound to my wrist under the water, but that was not the Charlotte that I knew. I had forgotten that there was so much more to her—that she had once been happy and smiling and care-free and alive—but then there she was, like a phone call from an old friend, to remind me.

"She's pretty," Casey said, as I leaned back against his chest to admire my work, momentarily forgetting that it was a painting and not a photograph. "You look just like her."

"My mom always used to tell us that people mistook us for twins," I told him with a nostalgic sigh, "but she was way prettier than me, and way more fun. Luckily, I got all of the talent though."

Casey laughed as we looked through the other paintings and I told him how Charlotte had posed in our backyard for that first one, and then in the studio at school for another, and at the park and the zoo and the beach...and how she had been a bigger part of my work than paint or canvas ever was, and not just because she had been the only person who would model for me. I also told him how she had covered the walls on her side of our room with my paintings, professing (not erroneously) to be my biggest fan.

"I can see why," Casey said, as we finished all the Charlotte portraits and started on the nature paintings. I unrolled a particularly good landscape of a flower-pocked valley with sapphire and lilac-colored flowers that I had seen on a nature show and then imitated with oil paints, and he continued, "Your paintings are amazing! I assumed you were good, but I didn't realize that you were *this* good."

I made another sound between a "pfft" and a "pshaw" and unrolled the last painting, the one that brought a whole new lump to my throat and returned the tightness to my chest that had just begun to loosen up.

"This is the last painting I ever did," I said, as if I had retired and died after a long, onerous career, "I called it 'Portrait of a Sunset'."

I held up the canvas and took in the bright, blazing orange sun and the deep, electric indigo sky swirled with pink, purple, and maroon clouds floating above a lush green field, pockmarked with flowers and grass that really seemed to be swaying in a light breeze thanks to hours of painstaking work with the thinnest paintbrush I had ever held in my hand. Miniscule mountains could be seen in the background, dwarfed by the enormous, spectacular sun that was setting behind them, reversing the natural order of the universe and making the mountains, for once, feel small. I had worked for more than a month on that painting, and had spent more than a few sleepless nights dreaming up the perfect blue-to-purple and orange-to-red ratios. It was my best piece, and it had been my favorite piece, but it, like everything else, had faded into nothingness the day I lost Charlotte.

"I think I know what I want you to paint in my garage," Casey said, his voice hushed with what sounded like reverence as he took the painting from my hand and held it up by the edges, studying it with the same strange, indecipherable look he kept using on me.

"Really?" I asked doubtfully. It was a good painting, but I wasn't sure that it was mural-worthy.

"Really," he replied, laying the canvas on his lap and looking me in the eye as he said, "This is the best painting I've ever seen, and I took an art-history class in college. This is incredible, Clara."

I shrugged uncertainly, blushing. "I don't think it would look quite the same on a wall,"

"You're right," he admitted, "but, then again, it could look even better. You're a fantastic artist, and I'm going to get you painting again if it's the last thing I do!"

I laughed. Surely he was joking.

"No, I'm serious," he said, taking my hand, "The world has been missing out on your talent for way too long. *You've* been missing out on it. I can see by the way you look at these paintings that you still love it. You've got to break through this block, and I'm going to help you."

"Well..." I said slowly, imagining what it would be like to have a canvas as big as a billboard and remembering how good it had felt just painting those silly little rabbits on that blanket a few nights ago, "I guess I could try it..."

"Good," Casey said, hugging me before kissing the top of my head once again, "Now we just have to go back to Home Depot and get some more paint!"

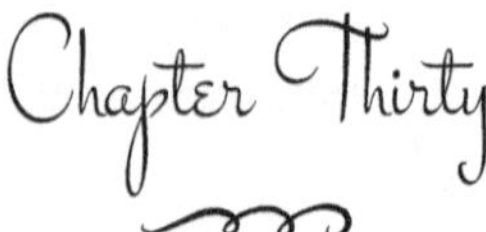

AFTER A WHIRLWIND (and regrettably dance-less) return trip to the hardware store, we made it back to Linderman's Garage bearing fifteen one-quart paint cans, a handful of off-brand brushes, and a ten-sack of White Castles for later.

"You know," I said thoughtfully, looking at the garage's shabby, faded façade, "We should get some paint and redo the outside too."

"What, you don't like the old, asbestos-flake look?" Casey joked, handing me the bag of burgers to hold while he carried the three flimsy plastic bags full of strangely combative-sounding paint colors.

"Oh no, *I* love it," I assured him, grinning as he attempted to balance all of the paint cans in the crook of his left arm while he fished for his key in his jacket pocket, "I just don't really think that your customers would."

"Maybe that's why I don't have any," he replied as I grabbed the loops of the top bag before all three of them could topple over and paint the parking lot instead of the wall. "Thanks," Casey smiled, leaning over to kiss me and reinvigorate the butterflies in my stomach before he stuck the gold key in the lock and opened the door.

My face burning, I followed him into the cluttered workshop, where I ran straight into him in the doorway and bounced off, nearly losing my balance and my burgers.

"Hey, what's the matter?" I asked, caught off-guard as he stood, as still as stone, three steps inside the garage.

"Where were you?" a small, plaintive voice squeaked.

Startled by the presence of another woman's voice in his garage, I leaned around the leather-jacketed wall that was Casey and saw a tall, painfully emaciated Native American woman in an ill-fitting black dress suit standing in the middle of the workshop area, which seemed to have been completely ransacked in Casey's absence. Drills, saws, and nails were scattered around the room, and the woman was still holding a hammer in one hand and a crowbar in the other, leaving us with no doubts about the identity of the vandal.

The woman's sunken, haunted brown eyes were wet and bloodshot, and her gaunt face was so long and lined that it was impossible for me to guess her age, not to mention her motivation for destroying Casey's garage.

I could, however, guess who she was.

"Mom," said Casey quietly, warily.

I glanced away from the thin, barefooted woman and up at Casey's face. I could only see his profile from that angle, but there was no mistaking it; he was nervous.

"I've been calling you for hours," Casey's mom croaked, her voice weak and her words wispy, as if they would break apart and float away like the paint on the front of the building. She dropped the hammer with a loud crack that made me jump and Casey put down his bags. "Where were you?"

"What did you need, Mom?" Casey asked, not answering her question. His voice was neither cold nor harsh, but it was clear that she was not a person he wanted to see.

"Can't a mother just call to check and see that her first and only living child is alright?" the woman returned, her eyes growing a bit wild as she ran a shaking, skeletal hand through her stringy black hair. It was a gesture so familiar to the one that Casey often used that it startled me to see it done in such a manic, frightening manner.

I put my bags down too, just in case.

"Well, I'm fine," Casey said, shrugging stiffly.

"I can see that," Mrs. Linderman snapped, shooting a withering look in my direction. "Where were you?" she repeated, while I attempted to make myself as small and inconspicuous as possible by taking a hopefully barely noticeable step back behind Casey.

"I was out, Mom."

"Who's the whore?" she shrieked suddenly, and though I was pretty sure she meant me, I hoped I was wrong, if merely for the sake of self-preservation.

"She is not a whore!" Casey barked back, his voice loud and strong this time.

Although I was growing more confused and scared by the minute, I had to admit that Casey's quick defense of my honor, even in the face of his obviously distraught mother, was yet another point in his favor.

"Don't yell at me!" Mrs. Linderman wailed, losing her anger and turning into a child-like wraith as she dropped the crowbar and burst into a fit of loud, sloppy, indecent-sounding tears.

"I'm not giving you any money, Mom," Casey said firmly, reaching behind me to take my hand, as if he needed to reassure himself that I was still there. I was glad to lend him my support, even if I was completely lost as to what in the world was happening.

"I didn't ask you for money! Why would I want your money?" she said, so fast that the words blurred together as she let out a loud, crazy, wicked-witch laugh that scared the living daylights out of me.

"You know why," Casey replied, moving away from the door and gesturing for her to go through it as he gripped my hand even tighter. "You need to leave."

"You don't love me anymore!" she sobbed, going limp and crashing to her spindly knees so hard that I swore I heard them crack.

"Yes I do," Casey said, not looking at her, squeezing my hand so hard that it hurt.

"NO YOU DON'T!" she shrieked, so shrilly that I felt the hairs on the back of my neck stand up, *"YOU DON'T!* You think I'm a slut! A home wrecker! A tramp!"

"Mom—"

"A bad mother! You think I'm a bad mother too!"

"Mom, please don't do this," Casey said, in a voice so broken that it made my heart ache. "Don't do this, not again."

"Well, you know what?" she asked, standing up, her skirt wrinkled and her hair wild. "I may be all of those things, but it isn't just *my* fault that your little sister is dead."

I glanced over at Casey's defeated eyes as she confirmed his greatest fear.

I had had enough.

"You take that back!" I demanded, dropping Casey's hand and stepping in front of him with an angry, protective feeling I hadn't felt before; a feeling that compelled me, for only the second time in my life, to step into a confrontation instead of out of one. "You take that back right now," I told her, jabbing my forefinger at her.

Mrs. Linderman looked stunned for a moment, her empty brown eyes wide, as if she couldn't believe my audacity.

"Neither of you is to blame," I said, swatting Casey's hand away as he tried to grab me. "The only person to blame is your husband, and he's not here."

For a moment, you could have heard a nail drop into the sea of hardware on the floor. Then, slowly, almost-sanely, Mrs.

Linderman took a step toward me. Then she did something that, in hindsight, I should have clearly seen coming.

She slapped me.

"What do you know about anything, you bitchy little whore?" she screamed, her breath hot and rancid in my stinging face.

Before I could react at all, Casey wrapped his arms around me from behind and pulled me backward, out of reach of the crazy woman. At first, I thought that he was purposely pinning my arms down so that I wouldn't hit his mother back (which, I must admit, had crossed my mind). Then I realized that he was protecting me. He was making a choice between us, and he had chosen me.

"Get out!" Casey ordered. I could feel the anger welling up in him as he tensed his body around mine.

"Casey, honey I—"

"GET OUT!" he bellowed, so loud that the walls shook, so loud that his mother and I both flinched.

"I see," Mrs. Linderman said, her eyes wide and red and knowing, "You choose her over your own mother."

"You're damn right I do," Casey said, holding me tighter. "Now get out of here before I call the cops."

The disheveled woman gave Casey one last lost, pleading look, and threw me one more hateful glare before storming past us, kicking over our paint cans and stomping over our White Castles as she hurled herself out into the early evening air like a swirling tornado, slamming the heavy door shut behind her.

Chapter Thirty-One

"I AM SO SORRY," Casey said, gingerly touching my tender left cheek. I had never been bitch-slapped before, but I must say that it was not an experience that I wished to repeat.

"She's a lot stronger than she looks," I joked, trying to lighten the mood as I rubbed my burning skin.

"Yeah, heroin'll do that to you," he replied darkly, taking my hand and leading me through the wreckage toward the back of the garage. "You'll want to put some ice on that so it doesn't bruise. I think I've got some back here in the supply room."

I trailed after him, thinking that the heroin comment explained a lot—his mother's wild, bloodshot eyes, her erratic gestures and mood swings, as well as her superhuman slapping strength. It also explained why Casey would have thought that she wanted money, and why he wouldn't look her in the eye.

"How long has she been like that?" I asked as he rummaged through a tiny silver mini-fridge in the back corner of the room where I had found Rosie's blanket.

"How long do you think?" he snapped back, slamming the refrigerator door shut and emerging empty handed.

I knew a rhetorical question when I heard one, so I didn't

respond as Casey brushed past me and yanked open the second of three doors at the back of the garage. I tiptoed over to get a look inside and saw that it was yet another small closet, barely eight feet deep. Instead of some sort of supplies, though, that room contained only a lumpy, bare mattress and a mess of empty Styrofoam Thorton's cups and Little Debbie wrappers.

I watched in silence as Casey stomped around what I presumed to be his bedroom, picking up foam cups and then tossing them aside before kicking a few more at the wall. I knew better than to speak. I knew what was happening. Casey was shutting down. One wrong word would set him off and I'd be back out on the street before either of us could realize that he didn't mean whatever it was that he would scream at me. I had to wait until the perfect moment to say the perfect words or I would risk being shut out of his life completely.

"Goddammit!" he bellowed, picking up one last 44-ounce cup and hurling it at the back wall, where it smashed, sending a thin stream of watery Coke sliding down the pale grey wall. "How hard is it for me to keep one goddamn piece of ice in this fucking garage?!"

He stood there for another moment, his big fists clenched as tight as his jaw. Then, just like that, his anger drained away and his shoulders slumped in defeat as he shuffled over to lean against the doorframe, his tanned face pressed against the painted wood and his eyes closed. I moved over to stand in front of him, still silent, still waiting for my cue to step in.

Casey opened his eyes and looked down at me, his lips quivering slightly and his beautiful brown eyes so full of misery that I wanted to cry myself at the sight of them. A single, solitary tear slid down his cheek and into his black beard stubble as he said, "Clara, I'm out of ice."

That was the moment I'd been waiting for. Without a single word, I reached up and put my arms around his neck and pulled his head down to rest it within the hollow between my neck and my shoulder. His shoulders didn't shake and he didn't make a sound, but he pulled me in closer and hugged me so tight that I knew, in that moment, that even though he was strong and brave and self-reliant, he needed someone like me just as much as I needed someone like him.

Chapter Thirty-Two

"SHE ALWAYS DOES THIS," said Casey. He had upturned an overturned metal chair on the less-cluttered left-hand side of the workshop area and had sat down heavily upon it, pulling me onto his lap. I had my good arm around his shoulders and my fingers were tangled in his already-messy hair as he leaned down to rest his cheek against my collarbone.

"What, destroys your garage?" I asked, surveying the wrecked room. Tools were still strewn all over the place, most of them broken, and the enormous toolbox I had seen before had somehow been flipped over. Mrs. Linderman may have looked wispy and frail, but she apparently had the strength of at least three large men.

"No, that's new," Casey muttered, "Usually she just comes in here long enough to con me out of some money and make me feel like complete and utter crap, then she leaves. And then I—" He stopped, tensing and lifting his head up to glance sideways at me, as if he had said too much and was hoping I hadn't noticed.

Sorry, no dice.

"Then you what?" I asked suspiciously, narrowing my eyes and leaning back to get a better look at his guilty face.

He looked at me for a moment, as if he were weighing the pros and cons of lying to me, then he sighed. "Then I go back there into the supply closet and bawl my brains out while I cut myself like an angsty emo chick."

My fingers stopped twisting his hair and I felt my stomach turn to lead. He looked ashamed, as if he was waiting for me to yell at him, but I was much more terrified than I was angry.

I took my hand out of his hair and held it out flat in front of his wary face.

"I think you need to give me your razor," I said firmly, trying to keep the anxious tremor in my heart from reaching my hand.

"My what?"

"You know," I said, getting impatient as my anxiety increased in proportion to the amount of images of past and future blood and gore that were flashing through my mind, "your straight razor, your knife, your scissors, your sword—whatever it is you use to cut yourself when I'm not around. You need to give it to me."

"Why?" he asked.

I was almost annoyed by his baffled expression. He wasn't trying to be difficult, he seemed to be genuinely confused.

"Because I'm not going to let you cut yourself anymore, that's why!" I exclaimed. "Do you think that I want to wake up one day and come over here and find you lying in a pool of your own blood? Because I don't!"

Casey's face softened as he finally realized that, unlike his mother, he had someone to help him, someone who would force him to be okay, someone who needed him alive and well and whole.

His brown eyes never left my face as he slipped his hand into the right front pocket of his faded black jeans and withdrew a narrow yellow Dewalt box cutter with a retractable silver blade. For a second, I was struck by how much damage such a tiny, unimposing little tool could do to such a mammoth-sized man. Then I quickly took the blade and put it in my own pocket, planning to safely dispose of it later when Casey wasn't around to see what I did with it. At that point, I trusted him with my life, just not with his own.

"Now you have to promise me something," I said, slipping my arms back around his shoulders as I looked into his eyes.

"Anything," he whispered, staring at me strangely, as if he were admiring some inner strength in me that I wasn't aware of.

"Promise me you won't find something else to cut yourself with if I'm not around to stop you. I have a hard enough time keeping myself alive, I don't want to have to do the same for you."

"I promise," he said immediately, reaching up to kiss me.

"Or take any kind of pills, even Tylenol, without telling me first," I said, leaning back a bit to stop him from kissing me before I had finished stating my terms and conditions.

He smiled.

"I promise," he repeated.

"Or find a gun somewhere and use it."

"I promise."

"Or a rope." I shuddered as the unwanted memory of Charlotte's dead body and purple neck bruise swam into my brain. "Especially not a rope."

"I swear," he said sincerely, without a trace of a smile this time. "I won't do anything to hurt myself ever again."

"Good," I said, reversing our normal roles and kissing him on the forehead, "because I don't know what I would do without you."

"You'll never have to find out."

Chapter Thirty-Three

IT TOOK us three and a half hours to clean up the garage, not counting the time it took us to eat our cold, flattened, dismembered White Castle hamburgers and dilapidated onion rings. After that, we were both tired and sore and a bit depressed, so, although it was barely nine o'clock, we decided to call it a night. Casey drove me back to my apartment on his motorcycle, and I stood in the doorway, fighting off a yawn and the uneasy feeling I had gotten as soon as Casey had suggested that we sleep at our own homes for once.

"Are you sure you don't want to stay here?" I asked, leaning against the doorframe as he stood on the top stair outside my apartment. "You can sleep in the bedroom and I can sleep on the couch," I offered, "I hate that bedroom anyway."

Casey smiled wistfully, threading his fingers though mine and tracing circles on the back of my hand with his thumb. We had already had this conversation back at the garage. Neither of us wanted to be apart, but what Dr. Jay had said about relationships forged in times of trauma had made us both a bit nervous. We didn't want to run the risk of our fledgling romance fizzling out because of too much intensity too soon, but that didn't stop me from wanting to be with him every second that I possibly could.

"You know I want to stay," he said, "but if we want this to work, we have to start off slow and let it build up over time. Otherwise, we'll just be proving Dr. Jay right, which is the last thing I want to do." He stepped up onto the landing and continued, "So I have to drop you off at the door like a regular guy would do after a regular date, and I have to kiss you goodnight here on the porch and then go home and toss and turn and think about you all night, hoping you'll still like me in the morning."

"And what if I don't?" I asked, trying my best to look pouty and upset when, in reality, he was becoming more and more attractive to me with every word that he said.

"Then I'll just have to come back here and convince you that you do," he said, leaning in to kiss me, softly and sweetly, before turning around and walking back down the stairs to get on his motorcycle.

"If I'm not here by ten a.m., you'd better come and get me!" he called up. Even in the dim light from the streetlamps, his grin still turned me to mush.

"It's a deal!" I called back.

He waved and I watched as he drove off into the night, looking back at me once, twice, three times before he was too far away to see me anymore. He wasn't even out of sight before I started missing him and, although I was tired from a long, eventful day, I could barely sleep. Instead of macabre memories of death and despair, however, I was buoyed by memories of Bob Dylan songs and motorcycles, slow dancing and soft, sweet kisses that made my knees weak and my head dizzy. I was falling for Casey hard, and I had stopped trying to catch myself hours ago.

As I turned over on the plush couch in my tiny apartment and snuggled beneath a blanket that smelled like him, I pushed down my uneasy feelings about being alone and I felt something I hadn't in a long time:

Happy.

Chapter Thirty-Four

I SHOULD HAVE KNOWN it was all too good to be true. I should have known better than to fall for someone whose life was just as screwed up as mine was. But broken people are desperately, involuntarily, almost melodramatically attracted to other people who are just as broken as they are. Fate or God or the Universe or whoever sees them as some sort of "matched pair;" as two broken puzzle pieces that not only repair each other, but complete each other on some deeper cosmic level. As hard as we try, we can't keep ourselves from falling for people like us, even though deep down beneath all the butterflies in our empty stomachs and the little pink hearts swirling around in our guilt-ridden brains, we know that it can't possibly last. To love someone is to make yourself vulnerable to the pain of inevitably losing them, but no matter how hard we try, we can't convince ourselves that it isn't worth it.

When I woke up that morning, I was still happy. I couldn't wait for Casey to come over, even though, somewhere in the middle of all of the tossing and turning I did during the night, I had decided that that day would be the day that I finally told him about everything: about Charlotte, about Davidson, about me. It would be tough, but I would do it.

Yawning, I got up and stretched, brushed my tousled hair out of my eyes (not without smacking myself in the face with my cast for the hundredth time first) and shambled toward the bathroom. As I passed the kitchen, however, something caught my eye and wiped the contented smile right off of my lips, murdering all of the goofy butterflies in my stomach.

The clock on the stove read 12:45 p.m.

Casey was almost three hours late. He had promised—he had sworn to me—that he would be there by ten and not a moment later.

Trying to keep calm, I went back to the living room to check the clock on the wall.

12:45.

I checked the VCR clock. The clock on the entertainment center, the clock in the bedroom, the clock on the TV Guide Channel, but they were all telling me something I didn't want to know.

I rushed to the bathroom and swept my hair into a low, loose ponytail, taking a split second to ask my panicked reflection in the landlord-replaced mirror if I was being crazy.

My reflection said no.

Without changing clothes, without brushing my teeth, without grabbing my stupid, flimsy, too-thin jacket, I put on my dingy shoes and ran down the stairs and out to the bus stop at the end of my street. After six and a half minutes of restless pacing, a rickety grey bus pulled up to the curb and I got on. I must have looked crazy enough to ride for free, because the driver didn't ask me for any money, which was good, since I still wasn't carrying any.

I rushed to sit down in the first seat I came to and began to bounce my cast up and down on my knee, trying to breathe deeply and convince myself that I was overreacting, that nothing was wrong, that Casey was just running late. He was fine, he had to be fine.

The bus arrived on Casey's street corner fifteen long, painful minutes later. Trying not to look like as frazzled as I felt, I leapt from the bus and walked briskly down the long, winding road until the garage came into sight.

Then I stopped.

There, in front of the garage and blocking the street was a horde of emergency vehicles: long, square red fire engines, sleek-looking black and white county cop cars, and a tall, blocky ambulance, all with their lights flashing blue and red and white as I felt my throat close up.

Before I knew what I was doing, I was running toward them, still hoping I was wrong, still wishing I was dreaming or that it was still yesterday and Casey was still with me, safe and sound and unharmed. I ran up to the first officer I saw, ducking beneath a long, yellow banner of caution tape. Before anyone could stop me, I grabbed his arm.

"What happened?" I panted, my eyes bulging out of my head and my heart pounding in my ears. "Where's Casey?"

The officer looked pained.

"You must be Clara," he guessed, his young, round face crinkled with distress.

"Yes, I'm Clara Halpert," I replied impatiently, getting a bit desperate, "Now please tell me where Casey is!"

"I think we should go over here and talk," he said kindly, before taking me by the elbow and trying to lead me away from the swarm of emergency responders.

"NO!" I shouted, wrenching my arm out of his flaccid grasp as I felt the first fumes of hysteria begin to fog up my brain, "Just tell me where he is! Just tell me that he's alright!"

The officer was tall and blonde and handsome, but I barely noticed as he looked down at me, his blue eyes pitying and somber as he said, "There's been an...incident."

"What kind of incident?" I asked, unable to breathe as the

pavement threatened to slip sideways and out from under my worn, faded, tennis shoes.

"Casey's been attacked," he said, putting his hand on my stiff shoulder.

"Attacked?" I repeated incredulously, "Attacked by who?"

"His mother, Estella Linderman."

My stomach dropped.

"From what we can tell, she waited outside his door all night, and when he came out this morning, she...attacked him."

"With what?" I choked, horrified. Surely such a feeble woman would have needed some sort of weapon to take down such an enormous, sturdy man like Casey, even if he was her son and probably wasn't fighting back.

"With a knife," he replied softly, as if saying the words quietly would make them less painful to hear, "she slashed and stabbed him multiple times in the stomach, arms, and face."

I was going to be sick.

"We think he was trying to bring you these," the officer continued, pulling a handful of long, stringy wild flowers out of his back pocket. The wilted pink, white, and purple blooms were tied together with a piece of white string and attached to a small, square piece of notepaper bearing one word: "Clara."

With my hand shaking so bad that I could barely hold it up, I reached out to turn over the card and immediately burst into tears.

"To my favorite Goonie," the card read, in Casey's scribbly, messy, handwriting, "Hopefully you still like me today. If not, maybe these flowers will change your mind. Love, Casey."

"He also had this on him," the officer said, handing me the wrinkled white napkin that I recognized as the list that Casey had been compiling of all of my likes and dislikes.

I could barely see through the hot tears burning my eyes, and the officer moved forward as if to hug me, but I stepped back, taking the flowers and the notes and holding them to my chest as if he were trying to take them away from me.

"Is he alive?" I asked the cop, my lips trembling as tears spilled from my blurry eyes down onto the unseasonable flowers.

"Yes..." he said slowly, uncertainly, "but it doesn't look good. He's lost a lot of blood."

"Take me to him," I demanded, a weak yellow pinprick of hope illuminating the empty, hollow place in my chest where my heart had been just moments before.

"I have to warn you—"

"I don't care about your warnings!" I screamed, causing several people to stop what they were doing and stare, unabashedly, as they watched the already-fragile girl that I was fall apart. Struggling to regain control of myself, I lowered my voice to a whisper, looking down at the cop's shiny, impersonal black shoes, too much like a funeral director's. "I don't care what he looks like, as long as he's alive. I can't lose Casey, not him too."

After a long, indecisive pause, the officer gave in and said, "Come with me."

Chapter Thirty-Five

OFFICER CALVIN "But you can call me Cal" Rookwood led me through a maze of caution tape and uniformed people toward the back of an open ambulance. I clutched Casey's flowers to my chest so hard that my cast dug into my left shoulder, but I didn't care. He had to be alive, he just had to be.

As visions of Charlotte and Davidson and the lake tried to transport me away from that new tragedy and into an old one, I heard a voice calling my name.

"Clara!" a thin, gravelly voice shouted, "Hey, Clara!"

I stopped and turned toward the grating, desperate sound. As soon as I saw its source, though, I wished I had just kept on walking.

"Hey, come here," called Casey's mother. She looked like a scarecrow, dressed in rags and tattered pieces of clothing that didn't match. Her black hair was frizzy and wild, but her eyes were wilder as she struggled against two large, muscular policemen who were trying to wrestle her into a set of handcuffs. She was covered in blood—Casey's blood—and I wasn't sure whether I wanted to cry, to puke, or to rush over and punch her in the face before my crime scene escort could stop me.

"What?" I snapped, my eyes narrowed and my fist clenched around the flower stems. The third option I had considered was sounding better and better by the second.

"Is Casey alright?" she asked as I walked over, Officer Cal's tentative hand on my elbow again, either restraining or protecting me, I wasn't sure which.

"Are you seriously asking me that question?" I demanded. Suddenly I was full of the familiar burning of a hatred that I had hoped never to feel again.

Mrs. Linderman was a mess, but even though I didn't want to see it, her brown eyes, so much like Casey's, were clear and repentant, and the desperation she felt was no longer that of a drug-addled fiend, but that of a mother who had already lost almost everyone she loved, and didn't want to lose the one person she had left.

"Please," she begged, her high-pitched voice like the whine of a dog, "please tell me he's okay. They won't tell me anything! I didn't mean to hurt him, I only wanted him to love me!"

I was confused, and she noticed.

"I had to make him love me more than you!" she explained in a loud, desperate shriek. "He's all I've got! I need him to love me!"

"So you stabbed him?" I asked incredulously. My hatred was beginning to mix with a sick sort of pity that I didn't like. It made me feel weak and afraid, and I needed to be strong for Casey.

"You don't understand!" she screamed. "You don't understand! When he came out that door this morning I asked him, 'Do you love that girl as much as you love me, your own mother?' And he looked me right in the eye, and you know what he said?"

"What?" I whispered, my voice small as Officer Cal's too-cautious hand threatened to pull me away and I struggled to keep my mind in the present and my fists away from Estella's face.

"'More'."

The broken wings of the butterflies in my stomach flapped feebly against the back of my throat as I thought about what Casey and I could have been—should have been. I was both crushed and elated by that single word, but more than that I was terrified, terrified because, once again, loyalty to me was costing someone their life.

"I had to hurt him then!" Estella was wailing, "I had to hurt him like he hurt me! You've got to understand!"

The two officers holding her tried to shove her into the back of a police car, but she resisted, calling out once more, *"FOR GOD'S SAKE, JUST TELL ME IF MY SON'S GONNA BE ALRIGHT!"*

"You'd better hope so," I replied, my voice steely with a threat I fully intended to honor, "for your sake."

Chapter Thirty-Six

A LITTLE MORE HESITANT TO guide me after my threatening chat with Mrs. Linderman, Officer Cal passed me off to an older, more distinguished, more authoritative-looking cop called Sergeant Loggins, who put his hand at the small of my back and led me over toward the ambulance.

We were approaching at an angle, and just before I could see inside the vehicle's open back door, Loggins slammed it shut and stepped in front of me, barring me from getting even a glimpse of Casey through the back window.

"Listen, Miss Halpert," the sergeant said, his Southern voice weary and his hazel eyes tough but kind, "I know that Mr. Linderman is a friend of yours, and I know that you care about him, but I don't want you to get your hopes up too high."

I felt like he had slapped me in the face, though his own lined, graying countenance was not harsh or mean at all.

"Casey's lost a lot of blood, and even though that doesn't mean he can't be saved, it *does* mean that you have to be prepared for an alternative you might not want to consider with right now."

"Why are you telling me this?"

"Because I've been on the force for a long time, and I've seen a lot of folks cut up like your friend there, but I've never seen one this bad. To be honest, I'm surprised that he's even still breathin' at all. If it weren't for the fact that he might not even make it to the hospital, I wouldn't let you see him right now, since you're not family. It doesn't look good."

"I've dealt with death before, and I can do it again," I lied. "Now can you just open the door so I can see him? Please?"

Sergeant Loggins gave me a long, sorrowful, "if-you-only-knew" sort of look. Then he sighed and opened the door.

Then I fainted.

Chapter Thirty-Seven

Unconsciousness is a funny thing.

Your body might be taking a break, but your brain is still working harder than ever, trying to make sense of how you came to be that way in the first place. My brain, however, took a different route. My brain rewound itself to precisely the moment that everything went wrong the first time, moments before it stopped functioning properly; the last time anything had made any sense at all.

I should not have been surprised to find myself, yet again, reliving the events of that day back in June. I was like a ghost, trapped forever between the past and the present, never fully able to commit my whole self to either one of them. A part of me knew it wasn't real, it couldn't be. But there I was, with the slick, wet green grass sliding under my new, bright-white tennis shoes as I ran from my mom's borrowed Taurus to the small, eerily familiar cabin where I knew Davidson was holding my sister hostage.

As soon as I had seen his painting in the art studio, I had called Charlotte—hoping, wishing, praying to God that she wasn't with him.

But she was.

It had been Davidson's cold, arrogant voice that had answered on the second ring, and it had been he who had told me to come to the lake; he who had warned me that if I called the police, if I told my parents, if I even glanced in the direction of a single other person along the way, he would kill my sister instantly.

I wish I had known then that she was already dead, that it was already too late. I wish I had known that she was already worlds away from me, that she was gone and nothing I could have done would have saved her.

But I didn't know that.

All I knew was that I had to drive two hours out to Echol's Lake on Little Randolf Road and do every single thing that my art professor told me to do or I would never see my sister again.

I reached the door of the cabin, which was ever so slightly ajar. My shaking hand hesitated as I reached for the rusted golden knob. I was no idiot, and I was definitely no action hero. I had called the police from an archaic payphone at a gas station I stopped at ten miles from the lake. They had promised to be twenty minutes behind me, but they had also told me to wait for them at the gas station and not put myself in danger.

I had disregarded that last part, however, and now I was having second thoughts.

My heart was pounding in my ears and my ragged breathing surely gave me away, because before I could even consider turning around and walking away, a deep, sinister, whispering voice was in my ear and a rough, oily hand grabbed me by the throat from behind.

"Aw," said Professor Davidson, his wintergreen breath blowing my hair, "Always the loyal sister, aren't we, Clara?"

I gagged as he squeezed my windpipe with his slender, vice-like fingers. I tried to kick him, but he slammed me into the wooden door and shoved me through it, sending me crashing to the hard, splintery, unvarnished wood floor.

As he closed and locked the door behind us, I coughed and retched and looked quickly around the room for Charlotte, but she was nowhere in sight. The cabin was empty. The roughly cut, raw wood walls were covered in hundreds of large, industrial metal hooks, from each of which hung a different gardening or lawn care tool. The cabin was obviously meant to be used as a storage or tool shed by the people who kept up the land around the lake. Now, however, it seemed to be some sort of makeshift art studio, with dozens of easels and tripods spread out like tents across the floor as the paintings they held were covered with blue tarps and white sheets.

Glancing back to the gardening equipment, I spotted a sharp, mean-looking spade on the left-hand side of the door, and wondered if I could reach it before Davidson caught me again.

"Don't even think about it," he said with a grating laugh, reading either my expression or my mind.

"Where's Charlotte?" I asked hoarsely, rubbing my neck with my clammy, trembling right hand as I used the other to drag myself upright.

"Ah, the million-dollar question," Davidson said with a smirk.

He looked different.

Though undeniably handsome in a spooky, vampirish sort of way, he had always looked a bit odd with his pale, waxy skin and his dark, stringy hair. Now, however, there was something about his cold, grey eyes that had changed. With a renewed jolt of horror, I realized what it was.

He was happy.

I had never seen him smile before, except for the day he had introduced himself to Charlotte, but he was practically dancing with glee as he moved around the room, humming a jaunty tune and unveiling canvas after canvas of dilapidated mannequin paintings, all of which featured a dummy-Charlotte in various forms of torture and/or dismemberment.

I cringed, fighting the urge to either vomit or scream, neither of which would have been helpful.

"Where is she?" I repeated tremulously.

He ignored my question once more as he unveiled the last painting, one of Charlotte completely whole and realistic, but hanging lifeless from a tree just outside of the cabin, from which a semi-accurate caricature of Davidson was watching with a sinister smile from a small, square side window.

"After Charlotte called me this morning to cancel our date, I got a little angry," he said finally. "I'm not used to being cancelled, on, you see."

I didn't know where this was going. Charlotte hadn't told me that she had cancelled their date. The last I had heard was that she was madly in love with him and consumed with a passion that I would never be able to comprehend.

"So, understandably, I was more than a little upset when she told me that, not only was she canceling our date, she was breaking up with me," Davidson continued, his pale hands clenched and his smile falling as he began to shake with a barely repressed rage. "Do you know why she wanted to break up with me?" he asked, moving closer to kneel down in front of me on the floor while I sat as still as humanly possible, not even daring to breathe.

"No," I said honestly.

"Because you told her to, you lying little bitch!"

In an instant, his hands were back around my neck, strangling me, choking the life out of me as I clawed at him with my fingernails, trying to scream for help.

"I asked her 'why, why are you doing this?' and she tells me that you say I'm no good, that I'm some sort of creep! She says that she doesn't know whether or not that's really true, but she trusts you—you're her sister, for God's sake! And she says she loves us both, but she could never love someone her sister doesn't like, because she loved you more than she could ever love any man!"

Though they were words that would have warmed my heart if uttered by someone else, I barely heard the end of his rant, for the blood had frozen in my veins at the word "loved." The rest of his paraphrase had been in present tense, but everything had changed with that one little word, that one little past-tense ending.

The room began to get blurry as he kept choking me, but he soon stopped, taking his hands from my throat and dropping me to the floor again, where I lay flat on my back, gasping and wheezing and realizing the terrible truth.

He had already killed her.

The police were still fifteen minutes out at least, and I was there alone without even a pair of nail clippers to defend myself.

"I never thought I'd be killing *you*, Clara Halpert," Davidson snarled, pulling a tiny key and a length of thin, brown rope from a cavernous pocket of his tan cargo pants. "Charlotte maybe, but never you. I've killed a lot of women, but I always draw the line at my students."

"But siblings of your students are okay?" I coughed with disdain, feeling the terror in my gut begin to mix with a feeling I had never felt before: hatred—burning, blinding, reckless hatred. The man had killed my sister, and he had just admitted to killing a lot of other people's sisters too—probably all women who looked like the mannequins in his old paintings. He was not only a killer, he was a serial killer.

Charlotte was already dead and I was next. Why try to cooperate with a murderer if it wasn't going to do me any good?

"You know," he continued, both ignoring and infuriating me, "it's a shame, really. You're actually a pretty good artist. Maybe almost as good as me! Too bad no one will ever know that now."

Without glancing back at me, he shoved the small, silver key into a lock on a door that was barely visible on the back wall. With some difficulty, I scrambled unsteadily to my feet, readying myself for an offensive attack. Charlotte would have wanted me to at least try to defend myself before I joined her in the afterlife, if there was such a thing. She had always been strong enough for the both of us, but now I had to be strong for myself.

Just as I was taking a step toward the biggest shovel I could see along the wall, he swung the wooden door open.

That time I really did scream.

The door had barely been cracked before something heavy, something limp, something monstrous crashed through it and onto the floor.

It was Charlotte—poor, beautiful, innocent Charlotte—whole and unbroken. My pretty white sundress pooled around her on the floor like milk from a shattered glass, and her blonde curls fanned out beneath her like chopped hair on the floor of a beauty salon. Her pale blue eyes were open, staring, bloodshot, and around her neck was a thin, purple-red line, the same width as the rope Davidson held in his slender, paint-striped hands.

"Charlotte," I whispered, tears falling from my eyes and onto her dress as I knelt over her, touching her clothes, her hands, her face. I had known she would be dead, but a small, childish part of me had still been holding out hope for some sort of last-minute miracle.

"You sick bastard," I growled, unable to see, but unable to look away from Charlotte's cold, stiff body.

"Funny," Davidson replied, though his tone implied nothing of the sort, "that's exactly what she called me when I tied her up and locked her in my trunk outside the art studio. She really thought I had asked her to there to 'talk about us'. Talk about naïve!"

"Stop," I said, sobbing now.

"She called me that again when I made love to her on the very floor you're sitting on. That was our first time, you know."

"Stop it," I begged him, squeezing my streaming eyes shut. I couldn't listen to anything more, I couldn't bear it.

"And she said it one last time when I slipped this rope around her neck and hung her up in that tree outside, just after I told her that you'd be next."

"STOP IT!" I shouted, leaping to my feet and striking out at him. But I was blinded and clumsy with grief and pain and he caught me by the wrists and slammed me against the wall, his pallid, skeletal face an inch from mine.

"She died begging me not to hurt you," he hissed in a sadistic whisper.

I kneed him in the crotch.

As he cursed and doubled over in pain, I rushed to the door of the cabin and flung it open.

But I couldn't leave Charlotte. She had died out of loyalty to me, and I couldn't leave her in the hands of that sick pervert any longer, even if she was already gone.

I raced back to Charlotte's body and tried to pick her up. She was skinny but I was weak from a life full of art and devoid of athleticism and I couldn't lift her. I reached down to grab her frail, stiff, white wrist to drag her out, but then Davidson hit me on the back of the head with something. Something hard.

I was still conscious when I fell across Charlotte, but he hit me once more at the nape of my neck and the world went black.

I wasn't out long.

I awoke just as Davidson was shoving Charlotte's beautifully lifelike corpse into Echol's Lake, and I gasped as I was pulled in with her, our wrists bound by the very rope he had used to hang her.

Together, we sank down, down, down into the black, murky depths of the muddy lake. The freezing water pounded against my ears and blocked out all sound. As Charlotte hit the craggy, rocky lake floor with a posture that seemed as if she was just settling down on the couch for a nap in front of the television, I noticed that Davidson had tied a large, black, fifty-pound barbell to her back.

There would be no escape for us now. She was dead and so was I. Dead because of something I had said, something I had done.

I wanted to cry as I looked into her pale grey eyes and touched her white face, the color of a china plate.

She was dead because of me.

I tried to swim upward, to scream, to cry out for help but I couldn't. I was bound to Charlotte by more than the rope around our wrists. She was my sister and I loved her with all of my tortured heart.

I looked desperately at her once more. She had always been my confidant, my mentor, my advisor; she had always been able to tell me what to do to survive all of life's trials and tribulations, however small and silly they had seemed compared to our present predicament.

But not now.

Now she just stared at me with her empty glass eyes and my waterlogged brain told me to give up, that it was no use, that I was already dead and that I deserved it.

My mind began to grow fuzzy as I tried to look beyond the emptiness in her eyes for something that I could speak to, something that would forgive me for being an idiot, and for being too late.

I whispered, beneath the water, beneath the waves, beneath the living world above, "I'm so sorry Charlotte."

My mouth filled with water but I didn't sputter.

It was my time to die. I had failed her, and now it was time to face the consequences. More than that, though, I couldn't imagine living in a world without my best friend, my sister, my Charlotte.

With a darkness that had nothing to do with the muddy water beginning to obscure my vision, I looked up at the surface to get one last glimpse of the sun.

"Clara!" someone was shouting, but I didn't know who, "Clara Halpert, can you hear me?"

I shook my head to clear it. My mind was playing tricks on me again. This was not how the story ended. No one had come to help me, no one had pulled me out of the water to safety. No one had called my name.

But this was a different story.

Suddenly I remembered the fountain in the park. I had been drowning then too, drowning in sewage and guilt, memories and remorse, and I had looked up to try to see the concrete angel one more time.

"Clara!"

I turned, thrashing in the icy water to look past the darkness, to see not that angel but the *real* angel, Casey Linderman. I knew if I could only open my eyes, he would be there, his shaggy hair wet and dripping and his brown eyes worried over me, and he would pick me up and take me away from all this, carrying me to safety in his big, safe, strong arms.

"Clara!" The voice called again.

I could almost see him now, standing over me, reaching for me. My heart lightened enough to keep me afloat in the sea of tragedy, and I reached out to him, to touch his tanned, scruffy face.

He leaned down then, his face close to mine, and I opened my eyes—really, truly opened them—to see that it wasn't the sun staring down at me, or a statue or an angel, and it wasn't Casey Linderman.

It was Sergeant Loggins.

Chapter Thirty-Eight

EIGHT AND A HALF HOURS LATER, after extensive surgery and one hundred and eleven stitches sewn throughout his body, Casey was lying in a hospital bed in the Intensive Care Unit and I was standing next to him. Although he was clean and pale and quiet now, all I could see as I looked down at him was the blood, muck, and gore that had been covering him in the ambulance. With a dark flicker of humor I recalled his intense aversion to blood and was sure that, if he had been able to see himself the way I did, he would have fainted too.

Casey had been heavily sedated, and was thusly deep asleep. I held his big, rough, limp hand firmly but gently, as if I were trying to tether him to the Earth while his mind wandered on its own in unconsciousness.

Hours passed like that: Casey lying still and unmoving, me standing faithfully beside him, holding his hand and occasionally sitting down in the rickety blue plastic chair beside his bed to rest my feet. The doctors had said that he should wake up soon, but the level of confidence in their voices didn't match that in their worried eyes.

Casey's stomach had been split open and his forearms had

been sliced to the bone. The jugular vein in his thick neck had been nicked and his left cheek had been cleaved open by Estella's knife, all of which had ensured a quick and painfully efficient bloodletting of archaic proportions. He had lost several pints of blood, and I had offered to let the doctors use some of mine to replace it, but we didn't share the same type. I desperately wanted to help in some way, big or small, but there was nothing I could do but sit there and wait, hopefully but helplessly, until Casey found his way out of his pain and his suffering and his own maze of tragic memories and came back to me.

Casey had always seemed like a giant to me—literally and figuratively. He was tall and broad, yes, but his spirit was kind and his heart was full of a compassion and a spontaneous vivacity that made him seem larger than life. However, as he lay in that bed, most of his long, jagged rows of stitches covered by a mint-green hospital gown and a thick, white, knitted blanket, he looked small and frail and weak. I recalled how he had held me all the times I had been weak, and how he had given me the strength I needed just to get through the next day, the next hour, the next moment. I thought about how he had grabbed my hand in the garage when I'd first met his mother, and I squeezed his hand harder as I remembered how he had squeezed mine then, as if to borrow some strength from me. I didn't have much strength, not anymore, but I wished I could give it all to him as he lay there, silently staring up at the ceiling through closed eyes. I would have given him every ounce of power and courage and life I possessed, even if it meant that I would have to sit back down in that stupid plastic chair and shrivel up into nothing myself.

I hadn't known Casey for long, but I hadn't needed to. He had come into my life at exactly the moment I needed him to, to be exactly the person I needed him to be. He had never judged me, and he had never let me down.

As I reached over to touch his face, white despite his perpetual Native American tan and marred by a long, thin, curved row of stitches that ran from his chin to his left eyebrow, I wished I could have told him what he meant to me. I wished I could have told him that I loved him and that I needed him, and that I needed him to keep on needing me too.

Struck by a sudden epiphany, I reached into the back pocket of my blue jeans and removed the list he had been working so hard on, the list that he had started so that he could help me to rediscover who I had been, and who I was now. I unfolded the napkin and placed it on the nightstand next to Casey's bed, where I also found his battered black marker amongst the other odds and ends he had had in his pockets when he left the garage. Beneath the rows and rows of Casey's crooked, childish handwriting, under the heading "Things Clara Likes," I wrote in huge, stringy, wobbly cursive letters: "CASEY LINDERMAN."

I left the list on the table, so that he could see it if he woke up, and I took his hand again. I leaned down to lightly press my lips to his clammy forehead, trying to put everything I was feeling and everything I was hoping into one single, wordless gesture.

Then he moved.

At first I thought it was a gasp of life or a jerk back into consciousness in a fairytale reaction to my kiss. I thought he was going to bolt upright like he had that night at the garage and call out for Rosie or even for me, but when his heart monitor began to beat a frenzied, earsplitting tattoo, I realized that Casey was having a seizure.

Before I could scream for help, three doctors and four nurses rushed in, shoving me aside, breaking my grip on Casey's hand and hurling me out into the hallway as I sobbed and begged and pleaded for them to let me back in, for them to save Casey, and for someone, for the love of God, to help me.

The door closed in my face but I watched through the tiny rectangular window on the side of it as the horde of doctors poked and prodded and pushed Casey's chest after strapping his arms to the white plastic bed rails. He flailed and lurched and bucked, but it wasn't him, not really. Casey was still far away, and I could no longer tether him to the Earth.

As I stood there, worthless, helpless, and crying so hard that my chest hurt, Casey gave one last, jerky lurch, then he was still.

The heart monitor let out one last, long, unending beep and I knew it was over; he was gone.

I had lost him, just like I had lost Charlotte.

Chapter Thirty-Nine

BEFORE THE MONITOR had been shut off, before the time of
death had been announced, I took off running. Down the hall,
down the stairs, down another hall and through the lobby, out
into the parking lot. I dodged honking cars and scandalized
hospital visitors as I ran, sobbing and gasping for breath, across the
sidewalk, the parking lot, the street. I had to get away from the
hospital, from Casey, from my memories, from myself. I had to
keep running; I had to make it go away. I had to find a place where
no one was hurt and no one was dead and nothing was my fault.

I ran down an alley, through a back road, over a ditch. I
jumped a fence and snagged my sweater and ran across someone's
backyard. I got chased by a dog and a kid and an angry driver. I fell
four times and tripped seven. I passed sixteen bus stops, seven
churches and twenty-seven staring pedestrians; I passed the park
where I got mugged and the Thornton's where I bought Slim Jims
and the street where I had realized that I was lost and completely,
dangerously alone.

I ran through the parking lot, under the caution tape and
through the open door of the flaky gray garage and fell to my knees
inside the place where everything had changed; where everything

had gone wrong again. I crawled, gasping and coughing, across the concrete floor, into Casey's bedroom and onto his lumpy, ratty mattress. I lay down on top of the purple blanket with pink bunnies I had given him and I hugged it to my burning, aching chest as I pulled my knees up into the fetal position.

As I inhaled the smell of him in quick, wet, ragged bursts, I knew that I could run forever, but I could never escape the memories or the pain. I could never escape the feelings I had for Casey, nor the enormous hole he had left in my already-broken heart.

Chapter Forty

Dᴜʀɪɴɢ ᴛʜᴇ ɴᴇxᴛ ꜰᴇᴡ ᴅᴀʏs, people came by and they told me things, but I didn't listen. They cleared up the crime scene and they went away, but I didn't miss them. I was alone in the world and I wanted it that way. I needed it that way.

I woke up alone. I went to bed alone. I spent every single minute of every single endless, miserable day alone.

But that was how it had to be. Recent events had proven that caring about me was dangerous, and I had to prevent anyone from ever trying to do it again.

The phone on the back wall rang occasionally, but aside from that the garage was quiet. The silence was heavy and oppressive, as if I were living in a tomb, which, in a way, I was. Casey's body hadn't been the only thing that had died that day. He had been the only person I had left in the world, the only thing worth living for. My sister was gone, my parents had disowned me, and now my boyfriend (could I even call him that?) had left me as well. My spirit was dead once again, and I didn't expect it to be resurrected any time soon.

Day after day I wandered aimlessly throughout the garage like a wraith, touching things and straightening others. When I got hungry, I ate peanut butter half-sandwiches made using the Wonderbread and the enormous jar of Jif I had found on top of Casey's mini-fridge. When I was tired (which was usually about eighteen out of the twenty-four hours in a day), I slept on Casey's lumpy mattress, covered by the blanket I had made amidst a sea of Styrofoam cups I didn't have the heart to throw away. I hadn't slept on a mattress (lumpy or otherwise) for months, and after just a few days in Casey's bed, the chronic crick in my neck was gone and I was almost annoyed by how much better my body felt when my mind was in such agony. I had been planning to lose all grip on health and sanity, to waste away into nothingness and fade away, but my body wouldn't let me. It made me eat, it made me sleep, and it made me wake up every morning feeling human. Worst of all, it made me keep being okay when that was the last thing in the world that I wanted to be.

On the sixth day after Casey's death, I was in the tiny, dimly lit bathroom to the right of the storage closet when I felt something rub against my leg from inside the pocket of my jeans. With the sense of an impending upsurge in my depression, I pulled out Casey's yellow Dewalt box cutter.

I remembered with a flicker of anger that he had given it to me with a promise that he would never leave, that I would never have to find out what I would do without him. I knew he hadn't meant to, not really, but he had broken that promise—the promise that had meant everything to me.

Like I had a thousand times before, I pictured his tanned face and his crooked smile, and I could almost feel the weight of his fingers on my hand, his scratchy kisses on my forehead, his thin lips against mine.

With a loud, grating, clicking sound, I flicked the lever on the box cutter and pushed the blade up and out of its plastic casing. Not crying, not sad, not even angry, I walked into the storeroom and stood over the large, rusty, metal sink.

I wondered how many times Casey had done the same.

I rolled the grimy right sleeve of my dirty sweater up without even the slightest hand tremor and lifted the box cutter. I looked down at my spindly, grubby white arm and saw that the perfect place for cutting, for slicing, for quite possibly ending it all, was covered by my stupid, worthless, ridiculously orange cast.

Frustrated, I inspected my cast for a weak point to chip away at. Then I stopped. All of my dark thoughts melted away as I finally saw what was really in front of me. The cast, originally a memento of my premier self-destructive episode, was covered in letters, in words, in scrawled and scribbled handwriting.

I dropped the box cutter into the sink with a loud, metallic clatter and sank down onto the floor, tears stinging my eyes as I read the different variations of the name I loved so much. I smiled as I counted the "Mr. Linderman"s and the "Casey Charles"es and the "C.C.L."s, touching each one with a reverent, quivering finger. I turned my cast over and over, taking in every single name, every single line of every single letter until at last I got to the part I loved the most.

"To my favorite Goonie," it read, in the middle of my palm where Casey's big, rough hand should have been, "Feel better soon."

Chapter Forty-One

I DON'T KNOW if it was the seemingly heavenly sign from Casey or the long, soul-purging crying jag I had afterwards, but that afternoon something changed. Instead of fitfully napping the day away, I stayed awake and tinkered with some of the power tools, trying to figure out how they worked and what they were used for. Instead of eating peanut butter and stale bread sandwiches, I ordered a medium-sized pepperoni pizza with some cash I had found sitting on top of the toilet tank in the bathroom. For the first time in almost a week, I washed my hands and face in the industrial sink where the box cutter still lay, ready for action, but as yet undisturbed.

That night, I still went to bed feeling depressed and vulnerable and broken, but less so than I had the night before. Seeing Casey's note on my cast had reminded me that he wasn't gone, not completely. He was still around in some form or another, just waiting to be needed, and so was Charlotte.

As I drifted into a restless sleep beneath the purple bunny blanket, my stomach churning with indigestion from eating the entire pizza I'd had delivered in one sitting, I thought about Charlotte. She had always been a strong, independent woman, and she would have wanted me to keep on living after she was gone, as would Casey. They wouldn't like me as I was then; they wouldn't want me to give up on myself. I couldn't bring either of them back by moping and crying—three months of lying on my couch after Charlotte died had proven that. I had to move on from it somehow. I had to let go of their memory, at least a little, and learn how to get through the day without them around, and without feeling like something I had done had killed them.

But it wasn't that easy. In order to let go of Charlotte's memory, I would have to finish the story. I would have to allow my mind to finish replaying that horrible day at the lake so that I could accept what had happened there and start to move on. In spite of the fact that I was rarely able to control the frequency and the intensity with which I recalled that day, I would have to let myself think about what I had done one more time, maybe even the last time.

Up until that moment, I had somehow managed to block out the ending, to keep myself from finishing the tale and admitting to myself what I had done. I had planned on going there when I told Casey my story, but since he was gone, I'd have to do it alone, just like I'd have to do everything else.

I took a deep breath and let out a heavy sigh, closing my eyes. I hugged the blanket to my chest, wishing it were a person with warmth and a pulse. Then I tore down the wall I had built to protect me from my own subconscious and I let myself finish the story.

Chapter Forty-Two

DARKNESS ENGULFED me as I floated, unable to rise up to the sunny surface and unable to sink down to the muddy lake bottom. I choked and sputtered as water continued to fill my lungs. As much as a part of me wanted to give up and die, however, another small, stubborn, primitive part of me clung to life with a desperate fervor that could almost be described as heroic.

It felt like my eyeballs were going to explode out of my face and the water pressure in my ears was so intense that I was fairly certain that it would crush my eyeless skull within the next thirty seconds but, in spite of all that, I was able to maneuver myself into a position from which I could pull myself down to where Charlotte was, using my own arm like a guide rope. The pressure in my head only got worse as I tried to weigh myself down by grabbing Charlotte's leg just long enough to inspect the rope tying the barbell to her back.

I poked and prodded with clumsy, wrinkled fingers, and eventually I found the knot. I clawed at it until my swollen, wrinkled fingers bled, sending a small, swirling trickle of crimson into the murky water, but it was no use.

I moved, then, to the rope binding our wrists. I didn't want to leave Charlotte alone at the bottom of the lake, but I promised us both that it would only be for a little while. A sick, possibly impossible plan was forming in my groggy mind, and if things worked in my favor, she would be back on the surface within minutes, and another body would have taken her place.

The rope was thin but strong, and I couldn't undo that knot either. The slender, braided nylon seemed to mock me at every turn as it encircled our wrists like a coiled brown snake.

I had been in the water too long.

Things had begun to take on the eerie glow of the surreal, and I had to keep reminding myself of what I was doing, that the rope was not a snake and that I was not, in fact, dreaming.

Beginning to panic as the real, true, one hundred percent reality of death began to wash over me, I jerked my arm in a desperate attempt to break the tie that bound me to my sister. The jerk had no effect other than to hurt my already rope-burned left wrist, but I jerked again and again and again until finally I heard a brief, muffled snap and I began to drift upward.

Confused, I looked down as Charlotte fell away from me, the bones in her once-perfect hand now broken and sticking out at odd angles as the rope that had once bound us dangled limply from my chafed wrist. I felt sick at the thought of having broken my own sister's hand, but I was free, and I was going to make it up to her.

My head broke the surface of the sixteen-foot lake with a splash and an explosion of too-loud sounds. As the water drained from my ears, I could hear birds singing and frogs splashing into the water, as if they didn't realize that a murder had taken place in their midst, and that another was imminent.

I coughed and spat, the water erupting from my nose and throat as I rubbed my eyes to clear them of the dizzy-darkness of near-drowning. As if for the first time, I looked at the brownish-blue water, the dewy green grass of the banks, and the tall, magnificent oak trees towering over me, their olive-colored leaves vibrant and lush against the backdrop of a clear blue sky and, for an instant, a millisecond maybe, I was glad to have escaped, glad to be free, glad to be alive.

But then it was time to get down to business.

As quietly as I could, I dog-paddled my way to the bank of the lake, my wrist stinging, my throat burning, my eyes still blurred by grimy lake water, and I dragged myself up into the grass. My clothes were heavy with water and I could barely stand on my shaky legs, but I got up and moved to the cabin, my sodden shoes squelching with every step and the knot on the back of my head throbbing in time with every beat of my heart.

Once there, I glanced around for the police who had already let me down, but saw no one.

Good.

I turned back to the cabin and crouched beneath the small, square side window. Carefully, quietly, I peeked through the glass and saw Davidson, just as I thought I would, collecting his paintings and humming erratically as he placed them in a pile on the floor, one by one. He was an artist and, despite their horrific nature, those paintings were some of his best work. I knew he would never be able to leave them behind, even if the possession of them would be more than enough evidence for the police to charge him and a jury to convict him.

Crouching, dripping, hating every molecule in that man's body, I crept around to the back of the cabin, searching for another way in. I'm not quite sure when my instinct for survival was replaced by an insatiable thirst for bloody vengeance, but I had nothing but violence on my mind as I reached the wide, door-less back wall.

I was not as graceful as I was vindictive, however, and I tripped over something on the ground, scraping my right shin and making much more noise than I had anticipated. Cursing under my breath, I glanced down and saw that the thing I had tripped over could possibly be the thing that saved my life. I took hold of the long, splintery wooden handles of the weathered pair of rusty hedge clippers that had been left to weather the summer in the grass, and I picked them up, feeling a hint of a malicious grin spreading across my once-so-innocent face.

"Who's there?" Davidson called, with some trepidation, from inside the small cabin.

A surge of satisfaction welled up in my churning stomach as I delighted in the fact that he was scared, maybe as much as Charlotte had been. Maybe more.

There were some thuds and scrapes as Davidson hastily snatched up what remained of his murderous art collection and I slunk around to stand beside the front door, hidden from view.

I heard him pick something up and move closer to what I assumed was the only exit, and I lifted my shears, holding them like a baseball bat.

Then my arms went limp.

What was I doing? I was no murderer! I was just a nice, shy, simple girl: an aspiring artist whose biggest crime thus far had been accidentally stealing a rubber bracelet from Walmart when I was ten. I had felt guilty over that for a month, until I had finally broken down and taken the bracelet back to the store with an anonymous confession note and a wrinkled one-dollar bill. If I couldn't live with *that* on my conscience, how could I ever live with the guilt of killing a living, breathing human being?

Davidson moved again and I tensed up.

Where the hell were the cops?

I knew it hadn't really been hours since I arrived like it seemed, but it had to have been at least half of one! And they had to have expected me to go to the lake without waiting for them—it was in the plot of every movie ever made!

I took a step back, away from the cabin door, and flattened myself against the wooden side wall, clutching the shears and breathing as if I had just run a marathon.

Everything had gone silent in the cabin.

Maybe he already left, I thought, without much conviction, *maybe there's another door I didn't see.*

Just then, someone grabbed me by the neck from somewhere to my right, pulling me backward with such force that they dropped me to the ground before I could make a single sound. As I hit the grass, the breath was knocked out of me as someone punched me in the stomach once, twice, three times.

I was dazed and in more pain than I had ever been in my life, but I also had enough justifiable rage in my system to strangle that bastard with my own bare hands.

As he quickly circled around to climb on top of me and attack from a better angle, I reached out and caught hold of my art professor's throat, stunning him with my ferocity as I began to squeeze his windpipe just as hard as he had squeezed mine before, maybe harder. He thrashed as he choked, scratching at my hands. His neck felt strangely warm and fragile beneath my fingers, like a rabbit's stomach with a quick, rapid pulse.

A heartbeat.

What was I doing? With just one twitch of my wrists I could kill that man, I could block his throat and stop his heart in a matter of minutes. I had never felt so powerful, nor so afraid. I was repulsed by my own intentions and for a split-second, I lost my nerve.

That split-second was all he needed.

Growling, he slammed me down on my back again and knelt over me, leaning down, his face a hair's breadth away from mine. He was so close that I could barely make out his crazy grey eyes or his pale, blotchy skin, but I could feel his anger, his hate, his pure murderous rage emanating from him in heavy, rippling waves as he put his hands around my throat to try to strangle me one more time.

"Nice try, Clara," he snarled, his spittle speckling my face as the world threatened to go dark again.

Just as I was about to pass out for the second and probably last time, I gave a great, squirmy lurch and flung him off of me with a kangaroo kick to the stomach. Before he could stop swearing and get up, I had grabbed the hedge clippers and taken off, running, tripping, sliding across the field toward the sound of police sirens that I prayed weren't just in my head.

But he was faster than me, he was smarter than me, and he was much, much angrier than me.

With no effort at all, he tackled me to the ground, punching me in the eye, the chest, the face, until, with an almost involuntary thrust, I shoved upward with my rusty metal shears and stabbed him in the stomach.

He froze instantly, his hands grasping for the spear that had impaled him. His eyes were huge and his mouth was agape as he looked first at the shears, then at me, as if he couldn't believe that I, Clara Halpert, his meek, timid, little art student had had the strength to defeat such a brilliant, maniacal, homicidal genius like him.

I pulled the blades out with a sickening squelch that made my stomach churn and he rolled off of me and into the grass, where he lay on his back, dark red blood bubbling and spurting like a weak, dying geyser from the enormous hole in his gut.

I rolled over too, and got to my knees, shears still in hand.

The sirens got closer.

Davidson began to laugh as a trickle of blood ran down his chin.

"What?" I demanded, my heart beating so hard that my teeth ached and my vision pulsed with every throb.

"It's funny," he coughed, smiling sickly, his teeth coated with blood that had risen up to his mouth from his ruined stomach, "Charlotte was convinced that you were the sweetest girl on Earth, pure as the driven snow. She used to go on and on about it. But the truth is, you've got a darkness in you, Clara Halpert. You're a killer too. You're just as sick as I am. Maybe that's why you're such a good artist."

He began to laugh then, loudly, harshly, arrogantly, and I felt my anger, my guilt, my overwhelming starvation for justice and revenge for my sister, my only friend in the world, fuel my strength and lift my arms, but he only laughed louder.

Gripping the upheld shears with both of my trembling hands, I gritted my teeth as a tear rolled down my face and I said, "I am *nothing* like you."

The police arrived just as I plunged the rusty blades into Davidson's heart.

Chapter Forty-Three

Needless to say, I didn't sleep very well in Casey's garage that night.

The conscience of a killer is never entirely clean, no matter how justified her killing may have been. I had learned that lesson well when my parents had rushed over to me at the lake that day as I stood, staring down at Davidson, covered in his blood and taking solace in the fact that he was just as dead as Charlotte was.

But my parents were stricken and sad, and had recently become hard-core Christian converts, so they couldn't see my survival as any sort of blessing. They couldn't be there for me when I needed them the most. I had broken the cardinal rule. The well-worn Bibles they toted declared that "Thou shalt not kill," but I haddest. I had killed Davidson, and I wasn't sorry.

I regretted the act of it, yes—I was never meant to be a killer. I didn't have the emotional strength to carry a burden of that magnitude around on my slim, timid shoulders, and I was much too innocent to have to know what it feels like to crush a man's bones beneath your blade and feel his heart burst in his chest like a thick-skinned water balloon.

But I had done what I had to do. He had attacked me, and I

had to fight back. He had killed my sister, and I had to avenge her. All the time I later spent feeling guilty and ashamed, knowing that I had sinned, that I was responsible for the death of one person and, perhaps indirectly, for that of another, would have been nothing compared to the fear and the paranoia I would have felt just knowing that my sister's rapist and killer was still out there in the world somewhere, living, eating, sleeping, breathing the same air as me. It would have driven me insane, even more so than I probably already was.

Davidson, it turned out, had had four other aliases and had killed seventeen other girls across the United States, so the police said (off the record, of course) that I had done the world a favor by taking him out of it. My parents, on the other hand, had immediately condemned me to Hell and kicked me out of the home I no longer wanted to live in anyway. Without a single word, I had dropped out of school and used my scholarship money to move into a furnished apartment a hundred miles from where I had spent nineteen wonderful years bunking with my sister. The apartment was lonely and sad, but it was better than living in a house where no one would look at me.

As far as my parents were concerned, they had lost two daughters that day.

As I removed my snagged, stained, smelly sweater and pulled one of Casey's signature red-checkered flannel shirts on over my pink lace bra, I wondered if he would have shared my parents' sentiments. Would he have thought me a brutal killer and a crazed revenge-freak? Or would he have thought me loyal and brave and strong?

As I buttoned a few small, black buttons over my chest, I wanted to believe that what Casey had said the week before had been true—that he wouldn't have cared what I did or who I was before I met him—but a tiny part of me was glad that I hadn't had the chance to find out for sure. Casey had died knowing that I cared about him, and I knew that he cared about me too, even if he hadn't gotten the chance to elaborate much on that.

I could see the sun rising through the filmy broken windows on the folding door at the front of the garage, and I decided that that would be as good a moment as any to start my life over. As the sun's first rays set the dim garage aglow, I realized that the only person I needed to forgive me or understand me or comfort me was me, and as difficult as it might be, I had to learn to do those things if I ever wanted to move on. It would be hard and it would take time, but I was tired of moping and tired of feeling sorry for myself and for people who would probably have forgiven me for the things I could never change anyway.

Stretching, I got out of bed and made my way to the bathroom, and then to the sink in the creepy store-room. With some difficulty and a lot of antiseptic-smelling industrial hand soap, I washed my hair and wiped myself clean with a rag that I had first checked and re-checked for little pink bunnies.

I felt a little better after I was clean, and even better still as I noted that the water hadn't made me cry. Turning around, I grabbed the mostly empty, gallon-sized jar of peanut butter from its place atop the humming mini-fridge and wiped a plastic spoon on my pant leg. I tucked the jar under my right arm and scooped out a spoonful of creamy deliciousness to munch on as I made my way out into the main garage area to try to figure out what to do with myself.

As I stared thoughtfully at the car lift and the tools and the dingy white walls, I noticed that the pale yellow sunlight was still filtering in through the dusty garage window and down onto a large, dangerous-looking electric Sawzall. Maybe it was sign that I should take up mechanics? I was apparently living in the garage now, why not run it too? All I would have to do was learn which tool did what and why. It couldn't be that difficult, could it?

Mildly intrigued, I padded over to the sparkling silver blade, my bare feet slapping loudly against the cold grey concrete floor. Taking another large bite of sticky peanut butter, I knelt down beside the device, frowning slightly as I followed the long, square edge of the yellow plastic casing and the jagged, sharp edges of the long, serrated blade with my sleepy eyes. I had no idea how to work the thing, and to be honest, it bored me a little. Soon, both my eyes and my mind wandered over to a small, rainbow-colored sunspot on the floor and I got lost in the smooth, circular shape of the light as it refracted off of the saw blade and onto the concrete in a brilliant display of nature's accidental artistry. In an instant, my mind went to paint and ideas about how I could get that pattern onto a canvas in a way that could even remotely resemble the intricacy of its model.

Then I had it.

I didn't have to start my life completely over. Like a crashed computer, I just had to restore it to a time when it had worked for me, a time when I had actually felt sane and happy and proud of myself. I had never felt more important, more passionate, more myself than I had when I was painting, and that was what I needed to do.

Shoveling another hurried helping of peanut butter into my mouth, I leapt to my feet and located the fifteen paint cans Casey had bought for me a week ago. Like a small, solid army, they were lined up along the baseboard, lit up by the morning light and the vivacious colors on the labels. I looked up at the enormous, blank, white wall above them: the wall on which Casey had wanted me to paint my largest masterpiece.

I put down my spoon and picked up a paintbrush.

Chapter Forty-Four

DECIDING what to paint was easy. Actually doing it was the hard part. I had never painted on such a large canvas before, and I had no idea how to start.

As I thought about it, I popped open a few cans of paint and stirred them with flat, rectangular sticks that bore the Home Depot logo and had come free with our purchase. The thin, watery dye swirled with its thicker, creamier counterpart as I mixed the paint to make it usable and rich. I got a splash of "Emerald Explosion" on the bristles of a large, flat-handled brush and stepped closer to the enormous wall.

As I reached out with my always-unsteady left hand, I bit my bottom lip, hesitating.

The question I had asked Casey at the store came rushing back to me.

What if it wasn't good enough? What if the scene I painted was not just huge, but a huge mistake?

I took a deep breath as anxiety threatened to drown me once more. I thought back to what Casey had said in response to my reluctance and lack of self-confidence. He had quickly, surely, confidently told me that, no matter what I painted, no matter how good or bad or ugly it turned out, it would be good enough for him. Charlotte had told me the exact same thing six months and three lifetimes ago. Even Davidson had admitted that my work was good and that I had a rare talent.

If they could have faith in me, why couldn't I?

With a halting sense of burgeoning confidence, I swept the wet brush across the slick wall in the first stroke of the first painting of the rest of my life. As soon as the deep, dark green hue made contact with the blank white concrete, everything fell into place. All of my doubts and fears fell away as I painted stroke after thick, feathery stroke of green until suddenly there was a field of lush grass where a wall of emptiness had been just moments before. I highlighted here and there with "Seafoam Surprise" and "Green Grenade," before eventually moving on to the vast expanse of clear blue sky, which I had to get up on a small wooden stepladder to paint.

I felt a little like God, creating the heavens and the earth out of nothingness, wielding only a brush and a vision. By lunchtime there was a field and a sky. By dinner there were trees and clouds, and by bedtime there was the beginning of a beautiful, breathtaking sun rising over a small, quiet cemetery where two broken people had once begun to feel whole.

Chapter Forty-Five

I DIDN'T SLEEP much that night either. The wheels of creativity don't stop turning because the sky is dark or because the clock says it's midnight. I gave up on the sandman around five a.m. and got right to work painting the scene I felt that I had been born to paint.

For three days I was a slave to my muse. I worked tirelessly—shading here, lightening there, getting up on the ladder, crouching down on the floor—until finally it was time for the finishing touch.

Before I climbed up onto the stepladder one last time, I took a step back to admire my work.

A proud, satisfied smile crept across my paint-spattered face as I saw the sun rising over the cemetery just as I had seen it that day with Casey. He had wanted me to paint a sunset on his wall, but I had had enough sunsets, enough endings. I needed to paint a new beginning, a better one, full of hope and light and promise.

The large, fiery sun (composed of a full can of "Blazing Tangerine" diluted by a bit of "Orange Outrage" and "Screamin' Saffron") rose over the grassy green graveyard amidst tall, sparkling trees and a sky full of more colors than I had a name for. The rich pinks, the deep purples, and the myriad blues all tinged the landscape with a mystical sort of light that shone down over the small, grey gravestones of three people I loved: Charlotte Ann Halpert, Casey Charles Linderman, and Rosie Estella Linderman, who had, not a headstone, but a tall, majestic concrete angel looking down on her.

Fighting the urge to cry for the first time in almost a week (out of joy or sorrow, I wasn't sure which), I stepped up onto the small but sturdy wooden ladder. Holding a can of inky black paint in the crook of my right arm and dipping my narrow brush into it, I began to write the word "Linderman's" in an arch above the rising sun, intending to make the mural into some sort of logo or advertisement for the garage.

Although several weeks with the cast had made me passably ambidextrous, it still took far too much concentration to form each of the big, bold, black letters. However, I was moving at a slow but steady pace until I reached the bottom of the last "n." As I leaned forward, my tongue sticking out between my teeth, to draw a line that matched the length of the one next to it, the too-tightly-held brush squirted out of my grip and fell to the floor with a clatter and a splat, mercifully missing my masterpiece.

Grumbling wordlessly, I climbed down to retrieve the brush. Completely forgetting about the can of paint clenched in the crook of my arm, I jumped as the cold, slimy "Black Dagger" paint spilled down onto the bottom right side of Casey's red flannel shirt.

"Crap," I muttered, trying to wipe it off with my hand, but mainly just rubbing it deeper into the cloth and smearing it all over my accidentally exposed stomach.

"Don't worry about it," called a voice from the doorway, "It looks better that way."

The paint can crashed to the floor.

Chapter Forty-Six

I COULD FEEL the cold black paint pooling on and around my bare feet, but I couldn't move them. I had been frozen, petrified, paralyzed by the surely impossible vision standing before me.

There, in the open garage door, tall and broad and shrouded in late-afternoon sunlight, was Casey. His left arm was bandaged from his wrist to his elbow and his right was covered from his fingers to his shoulder blade, which was bare despite the chilly October air as he wore only his white tank and ripped jeans. There was a long, thin, strip of gauze beginning around his Adam's apple and disappearing beneath the crusty, bloody collar of his shirt, which had been slashed across the stomach, revealing even more white bandages on his abdomen.

But it was his face that I couldn't stop staring at. His beautiful, tan, scruffy face was the same as it ever was, save for a long, jagged line of crisscrossing black stitches on his left cheek that curved up from his jaw to the far side of his dark eyebrow.

As he grinned that silly, sweet, irresistibly adorable grin that had always given me butterflies, I shook my head slowly, feeling a bit faint. This couldn't be happening. He couldn't be real. He had died in the hospital ten days ago—I had been there, I had seen it happen. I had heard the machine flat-line.

The irrational part of my brain suggested that maybe he was a ghost, or some kind of mirage, maybe even a hallucination born of paint fumes and too many nights alone in the creepy, lonely garage. But if any of that were true, and I really was imagining him, why was he broken? Why was he hurt? Why hadn't I imagined him whole and full of life, the way he used to be? It didn't make sense.

Still grinning boyishly, Casey pointed up at my mural and spoke once more.

"I told you I'd get you to paint again," he said proudly.

I didn't respond. I was still trying to figure out what was happening, why the universe was playing such a cruel and vicious trick on me.

His smile finally faltered and he took a step closer to me, limping a little as he looked me over from my messy hair to my bare, blackened toes.

"Damn, that shirt looks good on you," he said softly, his voice hoarse.

"You can't be here," I replied, my lips numb and my voice gruff from disuse.

"Why not?" he asked, looking back up at my eyes instead of the three buttons I had buttoned over my flannel-covered breasts, "It's my garage."

"But you're dead," I told him, shaking my head and taking a step backward, slipping a bit in the wet paint on the floor, "You died ten days ago in the hospital, I saw you."

Casey took a deep breath, looking pained. "You're right. I did die."

I was going to vomit.

I had seen *The Twilight Zone* and *Pet Sematary* enough times to know that a reanimated corpse or a ghost was bad news, even if it was so beautiful that it made your heart ache, even if it seemed so real that you were fully ready to throw logic and sanity to the wind and let your imagination take you wherever it wanted, as long as the ghost got to come too.

"I was legally dead for three minutes," he continued, looking down at the floor, his face blanching a bit in the dim garage lighting, "and then again for another two. But they brought me back both times with those weird electric paddle things."

"Defibrillators?" I suggested, much too loudly, as my throat threatened to close up.

He nodded, taking another tentative step toward me. "They tried to tell you what happened, but when they went out to look for you in the hallway, you were gone."

"I ran away," I said, feeling more feverish than faint now. "I thought you were..." I could no longer say the word. I could no longer say it if it was no longer true.

"I know," Casey replied, taking one more step toward me, his big black boots entering the puddle of black paint. "I'm so sorry Clara. I promised that I'd never leave you, and then this happens."

"You shouldn't have gone home that night," I said, shaking my head as hot tears made their way to my eyes for the first time in three whole days, "I had a bad feeling about it, I shouldn't have let you leave my apartment."

"Hey, it's not your fault," Casey said forcefully, the tips of his boots now touching my cold, bare, black toes. "If it's anyone's fault, it's mine. I should have known that my mom would come back. She always comes back. But none of that matters anymore," he said, reaching out to brush a tear away as it slid down my burning cheek. "I promised you that you'd never have to find out what you'd do without me, and I broke that promise. But now I fully intend to spend the rest of my life making it up to you." He paused, looking suddenly bashful and uncertain, "That is, if you'll let me."

I stared at him for a moment, taking in his big, dolefully-hopeful brown eyes. Then, before I could stop myself, I blurted, "I ate all of your peanut butter!"

"What?" he asked, baffled.

"While you were gone, I ate all your peanut butter and most of your bread," I said quickly, wishing I could clamp my hands over my mouth. My brain was telling me to shut up, but my mouth wouldn't listen. "And I spent all of your toilet money too, mostly on pizza. But I thought you weren't coming back, see, so I—"

Whatever I was going to say next was lost forever as he leaned down and kissed me, wiping out any doubts I had that he was alive and real and mine, all mine.

As he held me close, his big, rough hand on my cheek and his thick, strong arm around my waist, I got the feeling that he had missed me just as much as I had missed him. As he kissed me deeply, passionately, almost desperately, I reached up to touch his face, to feel the stubble on his chin, the hot, flushed skin of his cheek and the soft, shaggy curls of his hair. As if trying to memorize him, I trailed my paint-pocked fingers down his face to his thick, beaded neck, where I accidentally brushed his bandage and he winced.

I pulled back, appalled.

"Sorry!" I gasped. How could I be so stupid?

"It's okay," Casey said dismissively, leaning back in. I noticed that his face was covered in black paint from my hand and I felt even worse.

"No, I hurt you!" I insisted. There he was, just back from the dead, and I was already hurting him. My insecurity came rushing back as I realized that maybe it really was dangerous to care about me after all.

He brushed a curl out of my face and smiled patiently, stretching what would soon become a long, thin, raised scar on his left cheek.

"You could never hurt me, Clara," he said, his deep voice gentle. "Trust me."

As I stared into his big, beautiful brown eyes again, I was struck by the urge to confess much more than the petty theft of some peanut butter and some cash. I had to tell him everything, and I had to do it at that moment, before I lost my nerve.

"Casey, I killed someone," I said abruptly, trying to squeeze myself out of his encircling arms.

He looked more puzzled than alarmed as he glanced warily around the garage, as if he thought I had hidden the body somewhere amongst the screwdrivers and power tools.

"Who?" he asked, his whispered voice conspiratorial. "Was it my mom? Because to be honest, I had half a mind to—"

"No, no," I interrupted impatiently, shaking my head, "It was the man who killed my sister."

"Your art professor?" he asked, his eyes darting to my face as he struggled to keep me in his bandaged arms.

"Yes," I said, the tears stinging my eyes again as whatever acceptance I had accrued threatened to ebb away, "He killed Charlotte and he tried to kill me by drowning me in the lake," I said hurriedly, praying that he wouldn't stop trying to hold me as I kept trying to squirm out of his grip. "But I got out of the lake and I killed him." I let out a shaky sob. "I killed him, Casey, and I'm not sorry. But I needed to tell you because I want you to know the truth about me, about what I did, about who I am."

Casey was silent for a moment, and I thought my worst fear was coming true as he slipped one arm off of my waist.

"I had to do it!" I insisted, suddenly wishing I could take it all back.

But I couldn't take it back, and I wouldn't. I had to make my own peace with it before I could expect anyone else to do the same. I bowed my head and said softly, "If that bothers you, then I guess I'll just go."

"Why the hell would that bother me?" Casey asked, so incredulously that I was startled enough to look back up at his paint-smeared face. "If you hadn't already killed that guy, I would have found him and done it myself!"

I didn't know what to say.

"Clara, weren't you listening to me at Denny's?" he continued, almost angry now, "Whoever you are, whoever you were, whoever you want to be is fine with me, you know that!"

"Really?" I asked, my voice small.

"Really," he said firmly, taking my sticky hand and rubbing his thumb across the back of it. "I'm in love with you Clara, you have to know that by now."

"I love you too," I replied without any more hesitation, without any more fear, without any more doubt.

<h1 style="text-align:center">Chapter Forty-Seven</h1>

AFTER THAT, I told Casey everything: what had happened to Charlotte, what had happened to Davidson, but mostly what had happened to me. He held me close as we sat on his lumpy mattress, his arm wrapped securely around my hips in the way that always made me feel safe, and I shared the poisonous, soul-siphoning secret that had been eating away at me for so long. As the story came pouring out of me, some parts tinged with anger, some with sad, quiet regret, I realized that Dr. Jay had been right. The more of my burden I shared with Casey, the lighter it became. I may have already begun to reconcile with myself, but it wasn't the same as letting someone else into the deepest, darkest part of your heart as they held your hand and shared whatever light they had with you.

When I met Casey, I was a shell of the person I had once been —or worse: the shell of the person I thought I should have been. But I had gone through Hell and had come out on the other side —twice. I had earned the right to be happy, the right to be free, the right to love and to be loved by someone else. It may have been Fate or God or the Universe that had brought our two broken hearts together, but it was our choice to stay that way. Getting over the loss of our loved ones and moving on wasn't Fate's job, it was ours, and we were going to do it together.

When I finished my story, Casey kissed my lips and dried my tears, and we walked out into the garage, my tiny, painted hand in his enormous, bandaged one.

"This painting is incredible," he told me, stopping to look up and marvel at my work as I carefully slipped my arms around his torso, "It just needs one more thing to make it absolutely perfect."

Before I could protest, he leaned down and picked up the paint brush I had dropped earlier. He dipped it in the still-sticky paint puddle on the floor, and stepped toward my mural.

I cringed inwardly as he moved with the loaded brush toward the beautiful tangerine sun than had taken me the better part of two days to perfect. I watched with a mixture of curiosity and apprehension as he reached up with his long arm to scrawl two more words beneath the square, blocky letters I had worked so hard to paint straight.

Grinning, he stepped back and took my hand, lacing his rough, wrapped fingers through mine as he kissed me on the forehead, his whiskers tickling my skin and making me blush. Then I read the phrase that he had completed with the same scribbly, messy handwriting that covered my cast; the phrase that made the butterflies in my stomach dance and the lump in my throat return; the phrase that summed up the past two months and the next fifty years in three simple, perfect little words:

Linderman and Halpert.

A Note from the Author

I hope you enjoyed reading this book as much as I enjoyed writing it!

As you probably know, reviews from readers like you can mean the difference between success and obscurity for authors like me. If you have a moment, please consider sharing your thoughts about this book on Amazon or your other favorite book review websites. This would not only help me as a writer, but it would help other readers in their search for their next book as well.

If you'd like to learn more about me and my books, visit www.jessicascottromano.com.

Thank you for reading!

About the Author

Born in Louisville, Kentucky, Jessica Scott Romano has been writing since she was three years old. After reading far too many books about grand adventures in faraway places, she was inspired to go on a few of her own.

She now lives in Italy with her husband and two cats, where she spends her days writing, traveling, and sampling every delicious dish the country has to offer.

You can find Jessica online at www.jessicascottromano.com.

To learn more about her adventures in Italy, you can also visit her blog at www.anamericaninitaly.com.